SWINGS AND ROUNDABOUTS

Damián Alvarez is a man targeted by the paparazzi. A top professional Spanish golfer, he's dynamic, wealthy and impulsive. When he meets Emma McKay he employs her to organise his travel arrangements and control the press. She accompanies him and his entourage on the world circuit, and, despite her resolve, falls for Damián — but then his one-time girlfriend shows up. Is Damián capable of real devotion to one woman? If so, which one will it be?

WENDY KREMER

SWINGS AND ROUNDABOUTS

Complete and Unabridged

LINFORD
Leicester

First published in Great Britain in 2009

First Linford Edition
published 2011

British Library CIP Data

Kremer, Wendy.
  Swings and roundabouts. - -
(Linford romance library)
  1. Golfers- -Spain- -Fiction.
  2. Private secretaries- -Fiction.
  3. Love stories. 4. Large type books.
  I. Title II. Series
  823.9′2–dc22

  ISBN 978–1–44480–644–1

Published by
F. A. Thorpe (Publishing)
Anstey, Leicestershire

Set by Words & Graphics Ltd.
Anstey, Leicestershire
Printed and bound in Great Britain by
T. J. International Ltd., Padstow, Cornwall

This book is printed on acid-free paper

1

She looked bleakly at the two trolleys, piled high with books. Emma had known it wouldn't be easy when Margaret was made head librarian — they'd both been short-listed — but she didn't reckon with Margaret being vindictive. Janette, the other librarian, pretended she was delighted. Margaret rewarded her, by channelling some of Janette's responsibility in Emma's direction.

Emma knew she'd have to find a new job; things wouldn't improve. She was sorry; she'd enjoyed the work. She'd already applied for work within travelling distance. Eyeing the books, she threw back her shoulders and her rich auburn hair bounced on her slim shoulders. She'd replaced her own share last night, these were Janette's, redirected her way by Margaret.

1

Emma's soft brown eyes skimmed the titles and she began to sort them, her slim fingers working swiftly as she did the accustomed work. She paused to refill the coffee machine, and the aroma filled the office behind the main counter.

It wasn't opening time yet, and the others hadn't arrived either. The air in the high-ceilinged rooms was stuffy. She pushed the first trolley towards the main borrowing section and opened one of the outer doors on the way. The air was clean and sweet, although the sky was loaded with grey clouds. She dawdled for a moment, glancing up and down the empty street, and at the straggly bushes bordering the park opposite.

When the first batch was back on the shelves, she returned to the small office and poured herself some coffee. Leaning against the counter in the main lending room, with her mug cradled in her hands, the aroma drifted upwards towards her quiet oval face. She enjoyed the moment, in spite of the depressing prospect of what the day might bring.

She started to think about the next batch on the trolley but was interrupted by the sound of running feet, and someone rushing up the steps. A tall, dark-haired man dashed in and strode determinedly towards her. He looked back over his shoulder, and his steps echoed through the room. Halting in front of Emma, he spoke briskly. 'I need to hide; from the press. No time to explain; it's important that they don't manage to find me.'

He was in his mid-thirties and extremely good looking. Emma stared at him and managed to utter, 'Pardon?'

Impatiently he repeated his request, 'Where can I hide?'

She'd seen his face before, but where? He was tanned, darkly aesthetic with angular features and intense dark eyes. She felt intuitively that he wasn't a danger to her, or anyone else. She heard more feet approaching and, acting on impulse, threw open the door to the small office and said, 'In here! Keep quiet!'

He needed no second invitation and brushed past, leaving a faint spicy tang in his wake. She pulled the loaded trolley partly across the door with its frosted glass inset. It was just in time. People stormed the building, brandishing cameras and microphones. She didn't need to pretend to be astonished by the sight of journalists jostling with each other. A few of them broke away to search between the shelves but most of them advanced purposefully in her direction.

'Where's he gone?' 'Which way?' 'Where is he?'

One reporter waved a notebook in her face. Emma hid her nervousness behind a screen of challenging words. 'Who? Do you mind explaining? This is a public library; and it isn't even officially open yet!'

Impatiently one at the back spit out. 'Damián Alvarez! He was only minutes ahead of us. He must be here!'

'Alvarez?' Emma now realised she'd hidden a well-known personality but she continued to look puzzled and fished for more information. 'You mean the golfer Alvarez? Why would he come here?'

One mealy looking man in a grubby grey raincoat said, 'This is the only place around that's open!' He rubbed his bearded chin. 'If he didn't come here, did you see him go past?'

He hadn't passed; he was in the office. She shook her head. 'No! Even if the door's open, I don't stand there watching!'

One man was observant enough to ask, 'What's in there?' He dipped his head in the vague direction of the office door.

Emma's heartbeat quickened; she stared him out. 'That's the head librarian's office; it's locked. No one goes in there without permission.' She continued. 'In fact none of you should be in the building!'

One journalist scratched his head,

and mumbled. 'The shops are closed; nothing's open for at least three hundred yards.'

With over-bright tawny eyes, she replied. 'What about the park? He could have gone there! Anyway, why are you chasing him? What's he done?'

They considered her silently, eyed one another guardedly, and turned in chorus. They stormed out like lemmings. The odd one or two who'd been searching between the shelves hurried to catch up.

Emma picked up her mug and sipped the lukewarm coffee as she waited for them to vanish. She toured the rooms, and closed the entrance door. Shoving the trolley and shreds of uncertainty aside, she opened the office door with a flourish. Her visitor was sitting behind the desk with a mug of coffee, one leg draped over the corner.

He gave her a slow smile. 'Thanks! I heard everything.' He got up and held out his large hand. 'Damián Carlos Leandro Alvarez is in your debt!'

Emma reached out and their hands locked for a second. There was sparkle in his jet black eyes. His square chin indicated determination and strong will; his eyes hinted at exuberance and sincerity. Any misgivings faded, even though she recalled some colourful articles about him. She crossed her arms, resting her slender hands in the crook of her elbows, and considered him. 'Would you mind explaining what this is all about, Mr Alvarez?'

He was very tall with the well-proportioned body of a top sportsman; he moved smoothly to the bubbling coffee machine to re-fill his mug. Emma had to look up at him when he returned to face her.

'I was with Lydia Maynard last night — ever heard of her?'

Emma shook her head.

'She's a widow; used to be the wife of one of the richest bankers in the UK.' He added casually. 'Rumours are that they hated each other's guts, but a separation would have been stupid, there was too much money involved.'

He took a sip of the black coffee and lifted the mug. 'This is good! Anyway . . . Lydia's husband had a heart attack last week and she buried him yesterday. Lydia is not good at playing the bereaved widow. She phoned, and invited me to a dinner party last night. I'd nothing else to do, so I went. To my surprise, I was the only guest, but the press turned up too. They hammered non-stop on the door and, foolishly, Lydia opened it. She forgot she was dressed in a black negligee, and very scanty underwear.'

Emma didn't blink an eyelid, though it took a lot of willpower.

He continued, 'I managed to close the door. Lydia started having hysterics, even though I tried to point out her clothing was wholly in line with mourning attire. She got scruples — for the first time since I met her. She was suddenly worried what her mother would say, if she'd end up in hell, and how she was going to explain things to her children.'

His black brows lifted before he continued, 'I hoped things would quieten down, but Lydia grew more agitated and the press continued to hammer at the door. Perhaps it was gutless, but I decided to make an exit, via the drainpipe. It almost worked, but a reporter spotted me. I shook them off long enough to reach a friend's flat, but they didn't give up. Some were still waiting this morning. And then I ended up here.'

He had a slight accent, although his English was perfect. Emma vaguely recalled stories in the press about the amorous escapades of the 'enfant terrible' of the golfing scene. The sports pages agreed he was a great golfer, one of the highest paid on the circuit, and the gossip pages agreed he led a colourful life off-stage.

She glanced towards the door and said, 'I see.'

His mouth curved into an unconscious smile. 'Don't worry about them coming back! Speaking from past experience, they won't.'

She was curious and fascinated. She asked innocently. 'Don't . . . don't you mind — about being chased by the paparazzi?'

His eyes were bright with merriment, and he played with his mug. 'Of course.' He sounded more serious than he looked. 'They've created an image that isn't true, but I'm rich, single and enjoy life. I'm a perfect target. The truth is, I live a very normal kind of existence — well most of the time I do — but they distort, and report inaccurately.'

She hesitated for a second. She could say what she thought; she'd never see him again. 'It's not surprising. They get bags of money for exclusive stories and photos. Take last night for example . . . It's not an everyday happening to have a dinner date with a social celebrity only a day after she's buried her husband — especially while prancing around in your underwear!'

He looked at her large topaz eyes with their long dark lashes. A wide smile cut his face in two. 'Lydia was in the underwear; I was respectably dressed. I honestly thought it'd be a perfectly normal dinner party. I don't know why, but these things happen to me all the time!'

Tongue in cheek he said, 'Perhaps I should go into a monastery between tournaments, just to confound the press?'

Slightly irritated because he was making light of it, Emma answered, 'Everyone needs a private life. The press think you're good for a story because you get yourself into bizarre situations all the time.'

He studied her face and the soft lines of her figure in the toffee coloured silk shirt. He liked what he saw and appreciated her intelligence and her steady gaze. 'You sound like Carmelita!'

Emma didn't want to ask who Carmelita was, so she didn't. She waited.

He continued. 'How can I avoid trouble? I attract it like the plague. What's your name by the way?'

She replied promptly, 'Emma . . . Emma McKay', and went on impatiently. 'You're not royalty or a celebrity but you're in the public eye. Make it difficult for them to locate you!'

He ran his fingers through his thick black hair. 'Lady, that's not as easy as it sounds. I travel from one tournament to the next. Anyone with a fraction of intelligence can work out where I'll be, and where I'll be staying. The press follow me around like blood-starved leeches.'

'Other celebrities manage to protect their private lives; why can't you? Stars do stupid things sometimes . . . ' He blinked, but didn't comment. ' . . . but the tabloids leave them alone because they usually keep a low profile.'

His olive skin emphasised the inky blackness of his eyes. Almost apologetically, he explained, 'I try to be inconspicuous, but the wheels start to turn from the moment I check-in. Half of what they write is fabricated, and the other half is incorrect. It's a no-win situation.' He walked to the entrance, peeped around the edge of the door and closed it again. His tall figure came back with long, purposeful strides. The midnight-blue evening suit suited his dark features to perfection. Emma understood why women were attracted. She concentrated as he continued. 'It seems to be safe for me to go now, but I'll give it a couple more minutes. You don't mind, I hope?'

'No . . . No, of course not!'

He glanced around the silent room, and said, 'I gather you're a librarian?' He studied the creamy skin and the rust coloured hair tumbling to her shoulders. She was clever and spontaneous, and she looked good into the bargain. Her eyes were brown with gold flecks around the iris and she had a slim, supple figure that curved in the right places. Her head was on a level with his shoulder. She used make-up sparingly, and that was pleasing. Most of the women he knew put on a mask every morning. He stopped his contemplations and listened. 'Yes, but not for much longer, I hope.'

'Why?'

Emma poured out her story. She found it easy to talk to him. He listened with interest. Emma hurried to add. 'Margaret is good at her work, I don't dispute that, but I didn't expect she'd start a personal vendetta. She can afford to be generous, but she can't forget we were rivals. I can't complain to my superiors; they'd believe I'm carping out of sheer resentment.'

He looked at her and nodded sympathetically. 'Difficult! Get a new job.'

'That's easily said, but not so simple.'

Looking briefly at the surface of his Swiss watch, he crossed to the tea-tray and put his empty mug down with a clatter. Studying her briefly, he said, 'Tell you what, if you can think of a sure-fire method of keeping the press off my back, I'll give you a job!' He gave her a warm smile. He picked up a note-block, scribbled down a telephone number and handed it to her. 'My mobile number! I'm here until Friday then I'm off to Wales. If you can come up with a brilliant idea, call me!' He gave her another smile displaying dazzling white teeth. 'Thanks again for rescuing me!'

In a haze, she returned his smile. 'You're welcome!' She watched as he walked towards the entrance, and caught him up. 'Good luck for your next tournament, wherever it may be!'

He nodded and exited — going back in the direction he'd come from. Emma watched until he turned the corner. Eventually looking back down at the notebook, she wondered if it really was his telephone number.

Margaret arrived shortly afterwards and asked, 'Have I missed anything special so far?'

Emma looked up from the computer. 'No, nothing in particular! Oh, yes, almost forgot, a Mr Hawkins from central office rang. He wants to talk to you as soon as possible.'

Throwing her coat over the nearest chair, Margaret whizzed through the numbers in the directory and was soon smiling down the phone at Mr Hawkins.

Janette arrived and grumbled that the coffee jug was nearly empty. 'You've finished a whole jug of coffee?' Without waiting for an explanation, she went off to get fresh water.

Emma looked at the big wall clock above the entrance door. Suddenly the day didn't seem so bleak. She thought about Damián Alvarez and mulled over a way to provide him with more privacy.

Next morning she received a reply from a firm she'd applied to; they'd nothing to offer her at present. Margaret and Janette were starting an all-paid 'refresher course' tomorrow. She'd have to cope with work that was normally spread amongst three of

them. Emma's decision to find something else intensified. Things wouldn't
improve.

★　★　★

She visited her parents and told them
how she'd hidden Damián Alvarez in
the library, and also about his casual
offer. 'I've been thinking, and I've got
an idea he might like. It's worth a try!'

They'd both heard of him. Mrs
McKay looked at her with a worried
expression. She was an attractive
woman in her early fifties with a smart
figure, short curly hair and good
fashion sense. 'Did he really mean it?
And according to the papers he's a
perpetual womaniser!'

Emma laughed. 'Oh, Mum! He
insisted that lots of things they write
aren't true, and somehow I believe
him. He's pursued constantly by the
paparazzi.' She shrugged. 'Don't worry.
I'm not special enough to end up as his
latest victim.'

Her father leaned back into his favourite armchair; his bushy brows were drawn together and his hands thrust deep in his pockets. 'Don't underrate your attraction my girl! I understand why you want to leave the library, but you might be jumping from the frying pan into the fire. I can't pretend that I like what I've read about him.'

Emma nodded. 'I'd leave on the spot if it got too complicated. Anyway, I don't know if he was serious. Perhaps he's already tried something similar.'

'Hmmm!' His leaned forward. 'Go ahead, if you want to try. You know we'll support you, whatever happens.'

2

Emma put the phone down. She'd called and explained how they'd met. After a second or two, he'd sorted out who Emma McKay was, and he sounded quite friendly. Emma explained that she'd been thinking about how to safeguard his privacy. After another pause, he sounded surprised, but said. 'Really? I'm leaving the day after tomorrow. I've a practice round tomorrow afternoon, finished about six, back by seven. We can't discuss it over the phone now. Can you come here?'

She had nothing to lose so she said, 'It won't take very long to explain my idea. Where are you?'

'I'm at The Spinning Wheel. Do you know it?'

'Yes, of course.' Everyone knew it; the only exclusive hotel in the area. Emma had been there once; the day Robert had clarified his detailed plans for their future, and she'd bolted.

'Right! There's a lounge bar off the lobby. I'll see you there about seven?'

Emma was glad she didn't have to ask Margaret if she could finish punctually. She'd hurry the stragglers out, and go straight to the hotel.

Emma looked around and took a sip of the orange juice. She leaned back against the leather upholstery in the alcove, and waited for his reactions. He made every other man in the room look second-class. It wasn't just his expensive clothes; Damián Alvarez was someone who'd stand out in any crowd.

He ran his hand through his hair and leaned forward to hook his cup and take a sip of coffee. 'I see. You handle all administration and move me out of expensive hotels into private houses?'

With slightly heightened colour, she replied, 'Yes, that's it in a nutshell. If you rent a house, it'll take the press a while to find you. Even if they do, they can't follow you across the doorstep. If you make detours, and roundabouts, there's a chance you'll dodge them for the duration. The house doesn't need to be next to the golf course, in fact, it'd be better if it's a comfortable driving distance away. You'd be able to do your own cooking, if you want to. You won't need to go out all the time.' She asked calmly, 'Do you . . . cook?'

He gave her a wicked looking smile. 'Me? Are you kidding? I don't know one end of a saucepan from the other. I prefer to cook my competitors on the golf course . . . '

He studied her carefully. ' . . . Pablo my caddy, and his wife Carmelita, are usually with me. I'm sure Carmelita would love to cook. Ummm! The prospect of some home-cooked food is not bad at all!'

Emma pushed for the goal post. 'When you go out, I'll find out where the most popular theatres, restaurants, discos and bars are, and give you a list.

You phone the one you fancy before-hand, or even turn up on spec. That should almost eliminate the press for a while. It will take time till someone recognises you, and informs them. At present, I suspect hotel employees spy out where you're going — taxis etc. and pass the information on! Money talks!'

He tilted his head and looked puzzled. 'Why should I phone? You could do it for me.'

'That would be a waste of time and money. You'd need to phone me, I'd have to phone the place, and then phone you back to confirm.'

He paused and looked baffled. 'Why all the phoning around when you're going to be with us!'

The words catapulted her mind into instant disorder, but she managed to hide it. She swallowed a lump in her throat. 'You mean I'd travel with you?'

Offhandedly, he replied, 'There's no point in having an assistant on the other side of the world, is there? If you're my trouble-shooter and organiser, you need to be on the spot.'

She looked down at her half-empty glass. 'But I'd be an added expense! I'd need accommodation . . . and transportation.'

Sounding complacent, he replied. 'When you rent a house, just make sure it has three bedrooms — one for me, one for Pablo and Carmelita, and one for yourself. Apart from an extra plane ticket there's no added expense. It might be worth trying. Will I save money?'

'Without knowing what you spend at present, I can't be sure, but I think so. I presume you stay in top-class hotels? If you stay for several days, add the cost of roomservice, meals, an extra room for your caddy and his wife, entertaining guests, the use of secretarial services, then a house would be cheaper — but you have to add my wages and flight tickets.'

He rubbed his chin. There was a shadow of a beard. 'Yes, the idea's not bad, but let me mull it over. I'll be in touch in a day or so. Give me your phone number. Oh, is there a boyfriend, fiancé, partner in the background?'

She held his glance. 'No, no one special.'

He nodded. 'Good! That's important; I don't fancy jealous men-friends making trouble. Even if you told them I don't spend my spare time chasing you, they won't believe it. That's how it goes, believe me.'

She held his glance. 'It's your own fault, you've got yourself a reputation!'

He shrugged, grinning. 'Your telephone number?'

Emma ruffled through her bag and gave him her card.

He shoved it into his trouser-pocket, and Emma wondered if he'd remember where it was. Perhaps he didn't want to refuse outright. She got up.

Damián got up too, and studied the woman opposite for a moment.

In the dark blue suit, classic white blouse and dark shoes, she was dressed smartly without any frills. The lighting shone down on the rich copper hair and creamy skin. She was very attractive and well worth a second glance.

He wasn't sure if he liked the idea of her under his feet all the time but she'd come up with a scheme that might be worth a try. He'd think about it and talk it through with Pablo and Carmelita; it affected them as much as him. He held out his hand. He remembered he'd promised to double her present earnings. 'How much do you earn? I promised you more, didn't I?'

His fingers were cool and smooth as they touched hers. She swallowed hard and told him how much. 'Yes, you said double, but I'm not greedy.'

His dark eyes were bland. 'I'll be in touch. Goodnight. May I call you Emma?'

'Yes . . . of course!' Her hand felt lost in his and she had the wildest urge to pull it away. 'Goodnight, Mr Alvarez!'

His eyes twinkled. 'Damián, please!'

She coloured and nodded briefly, before she turned and left.

★ ★ ★

Three weeks later, she left the library. Damián gave her a laptop, his list of competitions for the coming months and an authorised credit card. Emma worked from home, and organised their first stopover, at a tournament in the USA. She felt apprehensive, but was confident she'd manage. She'd soon be jetting around the world, even if it wasn't on her own money!

They flew to Boston and caught a connecting flight to Denver. Emma had arranged for a rental car; her name was on the contract. The petite blond behind the desk looked up from the paperwork and her glance lingered on Damián. True to form, he gave her a generous smile. Busily scribbling on the papers, she informed. 'Additional drivers have to be listed and they cost extra.'

Emma put down her own driving licence and those of D Alvarez, and P Ramirez. 'For the three of us, please.'

She added the credit card.

The girl wore a smart navy-blue uniform with touches of gold. She nodded, picked up the documents, after a perfunctory glance, and noting the details, she handed them back. Clearly, she was not a golf fan.

Formalities completed, they collected the car. Damián drove, with Pablo next to him. They left the airport and drove into the countryside. Emma studied the passing Colorado scenery; it was a lot greener than she'd imagined. The hatchback had a GPS system, so Damián left guidance to an anonymous woman who gave him directions in a sexy drawl. Emma was tired even though the car's air-conditioning helped. She looked forward to a shower and some sleep, but she had to sort out their accommodation first.

Pablo had been with Damián for a long time. Now in his early forties, he was an easy-going, gentle man with twinkling eyes, tanned complexion and slightly bow-legged. He came from a family of wine growers living close to the golf-course where he'd caddied for Damián in his first important tournament. They'd stuck together, and Pablo had soon harvested enough money to live in comfort among his vines, but he enjoyed the life, and decided to stay with Damián. Damián shot to the top of the world ratings fast.

Emma liked Pablo; he had a calming effect on Damián. He was a rock in the storm and nothing seemed to shake him. Luckily Carmelita and Damián got on, even though Carmelita's mothering instincts irritated him. She was a comfortable figure. She was bubbly, chatty, lively and friendly. She had blue-black hair pulled back into a tamed bun at the nape of her neck and jet-like eyes that twinkled out of a dark-complexioned face. She chose her clothes for comfort, and sometimes she looked like an out-of-work musician as her clothes fluttered round her and her gypsy earrings jingled in tune with the rows of silver bracelets on her arms.

Pablo and Carmelita were a close, and loving couple. The only cloud on their horizon was the fact that they had no children, but they were philosophical and accepted it as God-given. At first Emma had difficulties understanding Carmelita's waterfall of imperfect English, but nevertheless she made Emma feel very welcome.

They drove into the small town and Damián stopped in the main street, twisting round to look at Emma. She needed a second to steady her thoughts. As long as there was space between them she managed, and felt in control, but when his face was close, she was very aware of his attraction. It was like constantly coming face to face with Brad Pitt, or Richard Gere — at any rate that's how Emma explained the effect he was having on her. Since she'd joined them, either Damián was making an effort to behave, or the newspapers had really exaggerated his amorous escapades.

'You have to pick up the keys here?'

Emma moved to open the door. 'Yes. From an agent's office on Main Street.'

Sliding his muscled sun-tanned arm along the back of the seat, he said. 'Look, why don't you sort it out while we go shopping? I noticed a big shopping mall on the edge of town. Carmelita knows what we need to survive.'

Emma welcomed the idea. Getting groceries was probably her job. If the others did the shopping now, she wouldn't need to drive back into town, and if there was no urgent email, she might be able to rest a while. She gave him a smile. 'Great! I'll wait for you here.' Emma got out and straightened her skirt, glancing briefly at the car as it did a U-turn and sped back down the road. Carmelita waved as they passed.

Emma found the agent's office and a few minutes later, the formalities were settled and she held the keys. He explained, 'It's only a few miles out of town — white pillars, ornate black iron gates — off the highway going south.

You can't miss it; about ten minutes from here. Someone went through it this morning so it's clean and waiting. Bring the keys in when you leave. If there are no breakages, I'll refund your cover as soon as I've checked.'

'Why is it empty?'

'The owners are on a cruise. They're friends, and I suggested they put it up for rent, but to be honest I didn't think they'd be lucky. We're a bit off the beaten track.' He looked over her shoulder. 'You mentioned four people when you made the booking; where are the others?'

Emma smiled. 'They've gone for groceries. They'll pick me up afterwards.'

'Well . . . Wait here! Where do you come from? My wife and I plan to go on a trip to Europe one day. My family originally came here from Italy; I'd like to go to see the place one day.'

Emma answered all his questions and told him she was a librarian. He didn't ask about the others. Emma was pleased; so far her idea was working. The golf course was within easy travelling distance, and if Damián was careful, it'd take a while for reporters to find out where he was staying.

The house was close to the highway. It had a pillared entrance-porch at the end of the driveway. The garden contained a swimming pool, and looked towards mountains in the far distance. They had all the privacy they needed. The men unloaded the luggage and Emma followed them inside. The interior was tastefully decorated and cared for. Carmelita and Pablo went straight up the winding staircase to choose a bedroom. Emma watched them disappear down a corridor off the upstairs landing. She looked around. Damián was exploring too. He opened the nearest door and looked inside. 'Hmmm. Not bad! Looks comfortable! I like the idea of being on our own after spending so much time in hotel rooms among strangers.'

'But, you're not on your own. There's

Carmelita, Pablo, and me!'

He gave her an unfathomable look, and closed the door. 'Oh, Carmelita and Pablo are family — and I'm getting used to you. This is working out better than I expected.' He came towards her. Reaching out, he suddenly pushed a strand of hair behind her ear.

Emma had the urge to jerk away. She struggled with uncertainty. It was an innocent gesture, but there was something about Damián that set alarm bells ringing. The articles about amorous adventures popped into her brain. She intended to keep things friendly . . . but purely professional. She looked up into his dark eyes. His voice was soft and persuasive. 'You look bushed! Go to bed!'

His consideration evoked an unexpected warmth in her. 'What about you? Are you not tired?'

'I sleep on long-distant flights. Flying gets boring after a while . . . ' He smiled.

Emma didn't comment; she'd already

watched him sleeping. Her lips were dry but she resisted licking them and nodded.

'It's not very comfortable, but you get used to everything after a while. I'll catch up on any deficits, tonight.' He swivelled her around and gave her a gentle push. 'Off you go!'

She looked back and asked. 'Do you want to choose your bedroom?'

He shook his head. 'As long as it's clean — and has a bed, I couldn't care less. Any one will do.'

Emma was surprised how casually he treated her; as if she'd always been around. 'I'll cope with anything after some sleep!' She walked determinedly towards the stairs and had to resist looking back to see what he was doing.

He was still standing and watching her until she disappeared from sight.

3

After a shower in the en-suite bathroom, Emma took some time out to view her surroundings. What luxury, and what a waste of space! Feeling a lot livelier, she went downstairs. She blessed easy-care materials that withstood the punishment of over-packed suitcases. Her knee-length skirt billowed as she skipped down the last couple of steps. Her dreams had been confused; Damián had been part of them. She didn't want to question why he was there, or why her dream-world seemed more desirable than reality. He was her boss — nothing more. Following their voices, she found them sitting around a shady table overlooking the swimming pool.

'Recovered?' Damián's eyes narrowed.

Emma fingered her hair and managed a smile. 'Yes, much better!'

Carmelita held up a pot. 'I've just made coffee. Would you like some?' She filled a gold-edged cup. Emma sat down and took a sip. It was wonderful.

Carmelita said, 'We're enjoying the peace. It's nice just to be on our own; a good idea. We'll have grilled steaks when the sun goes down!'

Pablo sat with his legs stuck out in front of him. He had a large wide-brimmed hat shading his eyes. 'We've been out to the course, to take a look around. We know who we're up against tomorrow, and it gave us a chance to check things out and work out a strategy.'

Emma settled back into the cushioned chair, and sipped coffee gratefully. 'And . . . everything's okay?'

'Damián has a tough partner, but no one he can't manage.'

'What time does it start?'

The legs of the chair scraped on the stone slabs as Pablo moved position. 'After the usual opening speeches — roughly ten o'clock.'

Emma asked apprehensive. 'You weren't bothered by the media?'

Pablo grinned. 'We went in the front, deposited stuff in the locker room, spoke to the organisers, and went out the back. If there were reporters around, we didn't see them.'

Emma nodded. 'I hope it stays like that. I'll start to organise our next stop-off tomorrow. The place sounds off the beaten track.'

Damián leaned forward, his hands resting on his upper thighs. 'It isn't; we've been there before. The town's in a real tourist area. There are bound to be lots of places to rent.'

Pablo stared unseeingly across the pool's turquoise water, and said. 'There are vineyards nearby.'

Damián looked up at the cornflower-blue sky with fluffy white clouds, and made a clicking sound. He studied Pablo indulgently for a second and then explained for Emma's benefit, 'Spain is pulling at Pablo's heartstrings again.'

Pablo laughed gruffly, almost embarrassed. 'Unlike you, I still feel a strong pull to the land of my birth.'

Emma could tell the two men got on really well.

Damián nodded. 'Wherever I put my hat is home! Nothing pulls me back, like your vineyard does you.'

Emma remarked. 'I presume you've friends and family in Spain?'

Damián straightened and then shrugged his shoulders. 'I've parents, a brother and a few good friends.'

'That's pretty good; some people don't have any friends or relations.'

Damián didn't answer. He got up, stretched his arms above his head and touched the overhanging roof. Looking at the garden, he said, 'Daylight's beginning to fade — and I'm getting hungry.'

Carmelita said cheerfully. 'That's nothing new! Let's get things started.' Carmelita shook out her wide skirt gave Pablo a knowing look and caught up with Damián who was on his way indoors. Emma heard him say. 'I'll help you chop up the stuff for the salad.' Carmelita nodded, and they went indoors.

Emma watched. When they were out of hearing, she said, 'What did I say that was wrong?'

Pablo leaned forward. 'Nothing really! He clams up sometimes. Damián's parent's wanted him to take over the family farm, and they tried to make him give up playing golf. They quarrelled when he turned professional.'

As Emma's brows wrinkled, he continued. 'I don't think they've ever properly patched things up.'

Emma listened with growing interest. 'But surely his mother mediated? Women usually patch family quarrels!'

'She supported her husband in the beginning because she thought he was right. When you believe the land is all and everything, it's hard to accept that times have changed.' He shrugged. 'Perhaps by the time Damián was on his way to the top, they'd drifted too far apart. Oh, don't misunderstand, they're very polite to one another but it's on the surface! Damián's younger brother, Julio, wanted to train as an hotelier, and his parents didn't stand in his way. They learned from the mistake they made with Damián.'

Emma still found it hard to understand. She sipped the last dregs of coffee and listened. Pablo shrugged. 'If Damián had chosen something with quick financial returns it would've been easier, but it takes years for a golfer to get to the top. They're years of living on a shoestring. It takes time and a belief in oneself, to climb the ladder. Success doesn't happen overnight. Lots of things can make, or break, a good player. I suspect the Elena episode held him up, but after that, he only had one goal — to get to the top!'

She was instantly awake. 'Elena?' That name was new!

Pablo ran his hand over his chin. 'I'm only repeating what I've heard. I know she was Damián's first great passion and the daughter of the local mayor. She was very beautiful; and very aware of the effect she had on men. Damián was infatuated, and eventually they paired up. Then Damián discovered another love, playing golf, and Elena, unfortunately for them both, didn't see a future in it.'

Emma's throat felt dry, as she waited for the story to unfold.

'Elena got impatient; her eyes started to wander. They finally settled on the owner of several factories. He was fifteen years older but his prospects seemed a lot rosier than Damián's at that time, so she dropped him overnight. Damián was shattered, and his game suffered for a while. In his home town, everyone knew about him and Elena, and also about his parent's opposition.' He leaned back and the chair creaked softly. 'I didn't know him very well then. He moved away, earned a living giving golf lessons and toured the minor circuits until golf took over completely.'

Emma's voice stuck in her throat. 'And . . . does he still see Elena? Is he still in love with her?'

Pablo lifted his shoulders and shrugged. 'Your guess is as good as mine, but I don't think so. I've met her once or twice the last couple of times we were in Spain. I don't know if it was coincidence, or if she was testing her luck. It's not difficult for her to find out when Damián's visiting; she lives close to his parents. She's still beautiful. If you're eighteen and your husband thirty-five that's acceptable, but for someone like Elena, if you're thirty-three and your husband is fifty, it begins to irritate you.'

'And Damián? How does he feel?'

He laughed softly. 'Your guess is as good as mine! He's a closed book. He's polite and they made small talk, but as far as I know, he hasn't attempted to see her. If he feels anything special, he keeps it well hidden!'

They jumped when approaching footsteps announced Damián's return.

Emma picked up a glossy magazine. Damián drew closer carrying a large plate covered in aluminium foil.

Pablo got up. 'I've seen the grill in the garage. I'll get it.'

Damián placed the dish on a side table. 'I'll help.'

'I'm not in my dotage yet!' Pablo argued, getting up.

Damián laughed; his white teeth flashed. 'I know that old man!'

The two of them ambled towards the back door to the double garage. Emma eyed them, and looked at the turquoise pool; a light breeze coming down from the hills rippled the water making diamond patterns on the surface. The moon was coming up and daylight was fading. One thing was certain, there was more to Damián Alvarez than anyone suspected. He wasn't just the carefree, insensible dare-devil people believed he was.

That evening was relaxing and fun. Emma was glad that she seemed to fit in without awkwardness and she was grateful that they all spoke English. The steaks were tender and grilled to perfection. There was crusty bread, a salad with lots of red peppers and also some delicious Spanish wine. Pablo said the quality wasn't so hot, but Emma thought it tasted fine. Later, they listened to the radio and made general conversation. Twiddling the dial Pablo found some Mexican music and it inspired Pablo and Carmelita to join in with some Spanish folksongs. They sang off-key but no one noticed.

A candle sent dashes of light across Damián's face, after an encouraging slap on his back from Pablo, Damián joined in. The temperamental music encouraged Carmelita to make flamenco movements with her arms and hands. 'Come on Emma, try — it's easy!'

Emma failed to copy with any great skill and with laughter in her voice, she said, 'This is impossible!'

Damián folded his hands behind his head and his eyes sparkled in the sparse candlelight. 'Probably anyone can learn if they're determined.' He leaned forward, and Emma saw his dark eyes sparkle in the sparse light. 'We'll take you up into the hills one day, to see some real flamenco.'

Emma's pulse increased. Damián Alvarez could be devastatingly charming when he chose. He was also a flirt, and not looking for a serious relationship. He was definitely not the kind of man Emma needed in her life. If she ever found the love of a lifetime, he'd have to be reliable, completely trustworthy and someone who loved her to bits.

Damián got up. 'I'm calling it a day.' He nodded at no one in particular and said. 'Good night!'

Pablo followed a few minutes later, and Carmelita didn't hesitate to take up Emma's offer when she said. 'Off you go, Carmelita! I'll clear up.'

Carmelita positioned her hands on her hips. 'Leave the grill; we'll use it again. And don't do the washing up! I'll do that tomorrow! I enjoy being in a house; it's almost like living a normal life.'

Emma smiled at her through the darkness. 'There's a dishwasher in the kitchen. No one needs to do the washing up.'

Carmelita made a disapproving sound and swayed indoors.

Emma lingered to study the dark silhouettes of plants and bushes in the garden, and up at a sky plastered with stars. She put the glasses on the tray and took them to the kitchen.

Emma settled down, and felt at ease. Damián's face flitted across the TV screen one afternoon when he gave a local TV station an interview; he handled it with ease. Emma was fascinated. Next day there was a picture in the newspaper of Damián giving autographs to a group of pretty girls outside the club house. He'd behaved faultlessly so far, and he even stayed at home sometimes and enjoyed TV or relaxed with a book; if he hadn't arranged to meet friends.

* ★ ★

The next stop was in an equally attractive house with its own swimming pool. If you hired a house of any standing in the USA, it always had a swimming pool. She began to enjoy everything to do with her job. She liked Pablo and Carmelita and she admired Damián's driving intelligence. She couldn't deny the extra spark of excitement of being with someone famous either. She'd proved adept at handling the work, and the press, and Damián treated her as if he'd known her all his life. Her confidence spiralled upward. She was travelling the world, had a lot of free time, and she liked the people she was with. Emma fed the press with as much positive information as they'd take, wherever they were. She reckoned it'd eventually pay off dividends. Using the internet, it took no time at all to find a suitable house, to hire it, to arrange for a rented car, and to organise the flight tickets. Damián had to defend his world ranking, but otherwise he was free to play tournaments wherever he liked. He was offered the post of an Ambassador for Unicef. Emma saw it as a heaven-sent opportunity to present a very positive image to the world; he decided his commitments might clash, so he asked to be considered later. Emma soon realised when Damián Alvarez tackled anything, he wanted to do it properly or not at all.

After this tournament, they'd move on to one in Ohio, and go from there to a Match Play Championship in Tucson. She'd completed arrangements for their stays and hoped things would work out as well as everything else had so far.

Emma was enjoying the luxury of sunning herself. Carmelita was indoors in the utilities room doing the men's washing. Emma discovered that Carmelita was never happier than when she was busy with housewifely jobs!

A shadow fell across her and she looked up. Damián was looking down.

She swung her legs to the ground and tried not to be bothered that his glance dropped from her eyes to her body in its red bikini. Steadying her thoughts, she managed to meet his eyes. 'How . . . how did the day go?'

'I birdied two of the last four shots for a one-stroke lead.'

She nodded. He tilted his head to the side and there was merriment in his eyes. 'You don't know what I'm talking about do you?'

She looked at him and her tawny brown eyes sparkled. 'To be honest, no, but I take it that you're not losing otherwise you'd sound different?'

He threw back his head and laughed heartily. 'It's very refreshing to be with someone who isn't golf-mad and doesn't pretend to be either. Everyone I know is an expert. I forget that you're new to this circus.'

'Do you mind — that I don't understand? Would you like me to learn what the terms mean?'

He shook his head. 'It's not your job,

and unless you plan to play golf, there's not much point, is there?'

In a tone that was apologetic, she said, 'I've never liked sport much. I was completely hopeless in school. I had to take part, but it wasn't much fun. I was more of a liability for any team than a gain. I like swimming and walking though.' She paused. 'So, you're in the lead?'

He looked amused. 'Yes, at the moment. That could change of course, but with luck, I've a good chance of winning.' He sat down on a low wall, with his back to the pool.

His closeness was like a drug, lulling her to a kind of euphoria. 'How long can you go on playing golf?' Emma took a deep breath to steady her thoughts. She inhaled the scent of nearby blossoming shrubs and sunned grasses.

'Until I die — or at least as long as I'm able to walk around a golf course unaided, but you're probably meaning to say, how long can I go on playing at this level of competition?'

She nodded.

'Your guess is as good as mine. I vowed I'd stop playing competitive golf when I slip down the ratings. I still hope I'll be strong enough to do that. I've always been very level-headed about investing prize money, so that shouldn't ever be a problem.'

'You enjoy it don't you; all the travelling and living out of suitcases?'

'Yes, up till now. As long as you haven't a shaky marriage because you spend too much time away from home, and as long as you're successful, it's a good life. I love the game and the challenge of beating someone as good, or even better, than myself. As long as I feel that, I'll carry on.'

He watched her intensely; she wondered if his gaze harboured a double meaning. Emma was embarrassed to find she was reflecting on what it would be like to be kissed by him. She felt a lurch of excitement but squashed it, and reminded herself that Damián was well practiced in attracting and seducing women. She blushed at her own reflections.

He brought her back to earth again. 'You look like you're enjoying yourself. I'm tempted to get some drinks and join you.' He appraised her with more than mild interest.

Her heart was hammering foolishly. Not wanting the situation to move in the wrong direction, she replied flippantly. 'Swimming with my boss is not part of the contract.'

He looked very surprised. 'Working for me doesn't prevent us enjoying ourselves, does it?'

'As long as things don't get too complicated.' Trying to sound casual, she avoided his eyes and added, 'I think I'll get dressed.'

He paused and answered stiffly. 'I'm not suggesting anything out of line. Perfectly innocent; a few lengths of the pool, a bit of conversation and a drink, that's all.'

Trying to ignore the heightening tension, she said, 'I'm merely being professional; keeping things neutral.'

His voice had a shadow of a sarcastic drawl. 'You're always professional, Emma. I've never known anyone who's more professional when I'm around. What's wrong with sharing the pool?'

'I'd like us to be friends because it makes my job easier. Anything more would spoil everything; we both know that.' She'd an urge to cover herself and scrambled to her feet. He looked up when she said, 'Let's not have this conversation; it's silly.'

Looking curious and chewing on her words, he asked, 'Why is it silly? I make an innocent suggestion, and you act like I'm about to drag you into my bed.'

Emma coloured and swallowed hard. She shrugged. 'I'm probably being influenced by all the bad publicity, but I hope you won't mind me saying that I'm happy to work for you, but I don't intend to get involved in an affair with you, or to sleep with you.'

Nonplussed, Damián was momentarily lost for words. He passed his hands quickly through his thick hair and then said smoothly. 'You're imagination is running wild. Nothing was further from my mind.' The skin tightened across his cheekbones. 'You seem to think my sole occupation, apart from swinging a golf club, is collecting women. Being professional, as you define it, doesn't automatically eliminate friendship.' There was a heavy silence. His eyes had an icy look. Glancing briefly at the pool, he added, 'I'll leave you to enjoy your own company.' He got up in a single motion. With a curt nod, he turned on his heel and strode towards the house.

Breathing fast, Emma stood frozen to the spot and wondered why she'd done it. Why had she acted like a brainless dim-wit? It was stupid of her to assume he wanted to conquer every female within his reach, and it was even more stupid to admit that old newspaper stories prejudiced her attitude. There was no reason to distrust him. He'd never made a wrong move, and why would he be interested in someone like her? She hurried into the house.

It was silent as she ran bare-foot upstairs. When she reached her bathroom, she splashed cold water on her face. Well done, Emma! You've probably blown it completely. You've practically accused him of being immoral when he made a perfectly innocent suggestion. She felt physically attracted to him, so she was acting like a complete hypocrite. More than anyone else, she should be ignoring all the lurid stories. It was her job to correct the wrong notions that had circulated for too long.

She studied her wide-eyed confused expression. She'd remain impervious to Damián Alvarez because as his assistant it was the sensible thing to do. Emma McKay and Damián Alvarez didn't mix. He may not be the Don Juan the newspapers tried to make him, but he probably did have short-lived affairs all the time. He didn't want to be faithful or true to one woman. She nodded to her reflection and told herself she'd only outlined how their working relationship should be. She'd over-reacted perhaps; with a tingling in the pit of her stomach, she admitted the idea of their bodies sharing the swimming pool, or lying side by side in the sun, made her heart lurch madly. She didn't trust her own reactions; that was the real reason she'd torpedoed things. She needed to make sure he'd keep his distance.

Emma tried to read but she skipped sentences and absorbed nothing. She looked at her watch and decided to get dressed. She chose an elegant short beige linen dress with simple lines, but decided it had too much cleavage. She returned it hastily to its hanger and changed into a patterned shift dress and low-heeled sling-backs. That looked better . . . safer! She decided she was glad she'd warned him she wasn't up for the taking. However attracted she felt, he was used to loving and leaving; she wasn't going to end up as a 'left-over'.

When she went out on to the terrace

their evening meal of succulent veal, mixed vegetables and rice was waiting, and Pablo was opening wine. The candle's flame danced across the sheltered walls behind them. Pablo poured wine into three crystal glasses.

Emma looked around. 'Where's Damián?'

Pablo loaded his plate and began to eat. Between mouthfuls, he answered with a shrug. 'He's gone; drove off like the devil was after him. We won't see him again today!'

Emma couldn't make up her mind if she was relieved or disappointed. If he wanted to make her feel guilty for anything she'd said, he'd be unsuccessful!

They went for a walk, came back to finish the wine and watch local TV. Emma liked being with Pablo and Carmelita. They were easy and uncomplicated characters — no hassle, no allures, and no complications. She was used to living on her own, but she liked being with them.

4

The distant hills were blanketed in morning hues of violet and blue. Emma decided to ignore the previous day. She may have annoyed him for a short time, but he wasn't small-minded. Unless he really wanted to fire her, he wouldn't give it another thought. In the kitchen, Carmelita was drinking coffee listlessly and staring out of the open window. She automatically filled Emma's mug with fragrant coffee.

Emma smiled. 'Thanks! Where's everyone? I just heard the car driving away. They're early aren't they?'

Carmelita rolled her eyes. 'Damián didn't come home last night. He just sent a taxi for Pablo to bring him his gear at some hotel. They'll go straight from there to the clubhouse.'

Emma bit her lip; did it mean trouble for her? She picked up her mug and said, 'I need to buy new batteries for my camera; do you want anything while I'm at the store?'

Carmelita looked thoughtful as she put two slices of bread in the toaster. 'Milk and some grated cheese.'

Emma nodded. Avoiding talk about Damián, she said, 'Have you noticed that Americans never seem to walk anywhere? They think anyone who does is mad! It won't take me long; I'll take a short-cut across the back streets.

Carmelita demonstrated that she sympathised with the American way of life.

Emma enjoyed the walk. The town's sidewalks were empty and there was hardly any traffic. At the cash-desk, she saw Damián's face plastered across the front page of the local newspaper. She picked up a copy, paid the cashier, and managed to wait until she reached the edge of the town. She stopped on the dusty road. There was a pleasant breeze, but Emma paid little attention to the gentle wind. It was fixed on some photos; Damián enjoying himself in a nightclub with some pretty girls.

A platinum blond had her arms wrapped round his neck, and a voluptuous brunette with full lips and metre-long eyelashes was sitting on his lap. The collar of his shirt was open and his tie was lost to sight. A second picture showed him on the dance floor, doing some kind of a snake-dance with the platinum blond.

Emma felt a surge of annoyance. She'd been employed to generate a more restrained image for the press. It was difficult to understand why he deliberately drew attention to himself — he could have gone out with these girls without attracting so much media coverage. She folded the paper angrily, shoved it under her arm and marched back to the house.

Carmelita was watering the plants. She followed Emma into the kitchen and took the brown paper bag containing the milk and grated cheese. Emma handed her the newspaper. 'Damián's on the front page.'

Carmelita viewed the photos and skimmed the article. Emma wasn't sure if she understood the colourful text — but the pictures were self-explanatory. Carmelita shrugged. 'I keep thinking he's learned his lesson, but I'm mistaken. Want it back?' She held out the paper in Emma's direction. Emma took it, rolled the paper into a tube, and threw it in the bin.

Emma decided to channel her annoyance. She opened some fan mail that had collected on his website, and composed replies for his reading later on. She began to search the internet for suitable accommodation for their next move and, after a short break for a sandwich-lunch with Carmelita, she began to study airline timetables. The internet was brilliant; it was all there at the touch of a button. Emma printed out everything, and put it into a folder for finalising with Pablo and Damián.

It was late afternoon, and the sun was sinking behind the far-off hills, when she heard the car coming up the drive. Emma was on the terrace re-reading the part of the book she hadn't understood yesterday. A few minutes later, Pablo came out and smiled a greeting. He threw himself into a chair, and ran his hands down his face. 'That's better!'

Emma asked, 'How did things go?'

He gave her a thumbs-down sign. 'Don't ask! He threw away the lead, and I'll be surprised if he pulls it around tomorrow.'

Carmelita handed him a glass of fruit juice, wordlessly. He drank it down in a single gulp. In her English, which was improving daily because of intensive conversations with Emma, Carmelita said, 'Not surprising, considering what's written in the newspaper!'

Pablo shrugged. 'It buzzed through the clubhouse all day, although his direct opponent was clever enough not to mention it. Damián took some gibes in the locker room before we left and some reporters shadowed us when we came out. I went back and forth through supermarket parking lots and down back streets to shake them off but it seemed to work. No one was following the last couple of miles.' He rose and added, 'It's his life; he's old enough! Sometimes I think he could enjoy himself as much without all the publicity, but . . . I'm off to have a shower now before we eat.'

Carmelita got up too. 'I may as well start cooking. I presume Damián will be in tonight.' She looked briefly at Emma. 'It's a . . . what do you call it, meat and vegetables mixed in a pot, in the oven?'

Emma added automatically. 'A casserole?'

'Yes, that's what it is — a casserole.'

Repeating the new word, she waved Emma's offer of help, and headed towards the kitchen.

Emma's book lay open, but the words were just mixed up black lettering again. She stiffened when she saw Damián coming. She was intensely aware of his tall, handsome figure and his beautifully proportioned body. His hair was still wet from the shower, and a faint lemon odour surrounded him when he reached her. He stood for a moment looking across at the strip of garden surrounding the pool. Emma could think of nothing to say, so she remained silent. He sat down in the opposite chair and she was forced to look at him. His eyes caught hers; he made no effort to say anything and Emma looked away.

His voice forced her attention. 'Anything special?'

She cleared her throat and struggled to maintain a conciliatory tone. 'The usual things; fan mail, schedules for approval, and your face plastered all over the local newspaper!' She took a deep breath. 'I thought the idea was not to attract attention? How did reporters find out where you were?'

His eyes narrowed and his back straightened. 'Your guess is as good as mine. Someone recognised me I expect, and phoned the press.'

'Pablo said they followed you for part of the way today.'

'Did they? I didn't notice. I was glad to close my eyes; there were fifty dwarfs hammering at my head from the inside.'

She gazed at him with what she hoped was a withering look. 'I hope you don't expect me to sympathise?'

His eyes flashed and he gave a crooked smile. He showed no signs of relenting. 'Quite honestly, I don't give a damn if you sympathise or not. I pay you to do a job, not to criticise. You have a pretty easy life, thanks to me, so I doubt very much if you really care one way or the other. You've already judged me, so it makes no difference! I'm answerable to no one but myself, and I take headaches and disastrous days on the putting greens in my stride.'

She couldn't fail to catch the sarcasm. The colour faded and then flooded her face and she plunged on carelessly. 'Are you being bad tempered because you didn't come out on top today, because of the newspaper reports, because you have a headache, or because of our conversation by the pool yesterday? I'm not responsible for the first three, but if the last one bothers you and you think I'm an unnecessary liability just say so and I'll pack my bags!'

She added as an afterthought, 'It's hard not to criticise you! The press went to town again, and you were the focus of attention — I've been employed to try to quieten thing down, but I can't do that unless you cooperate and make yourself less conspicuous!' She got up. 'If you're in a bad mood take it out on the press, or your latest girlfriends, but not me; I'm just doing my job.'

His mouth was a thin line and his eyes gleamed like volcanic rock.

Carmelita had mentioned that he had a volatile Spanish temper and Emma didn't want to give him time to explode. She said stiffly, 'I'll leave you to enjoy some peace and quiet; you obviously need some!'

She hurried inside and her determination almost faltered, but by the time she reached her room, she'd swallowed most of her annoyance and wished she hadn't left her book behind. She stretched out on the bed and linked her fingers behind her head. Her light brown eyebrows wrinkled as she recalled what they'd said. Perhaps he'd really sack her now. If he threw her out on her ear, she'd have to live from her meagre savings for a while until she found something else.

On the terrace, Damián found it impossible not to let a smile ruffle his mouth. She was a cool character, but determined. She didn't let anyone walk roughshod over her and didn't pander to his ego either. He picked up her book, looked at the front and back cover, and put it down again. Staring into space for a few seconds, he decided to make his peace with Carmelita by offering to help with the evening meal. Perhaps she had a bottle of aspirin.

Emma heard Carmelita's laughter

before she entered the room. Damián looked up and said smoothly, 'Ah, Emma! A glass of wine before dinner? Would you like red or white?'

She sat down, her thin fingers laced in her lap. 'White, please.'

She watched him as he filled a long-stemmed crystal glass, and was relieved to note there was no vexation in his voice. She was taken aback when he said, 'My headache's a lot better and my mood is too. I'd no intention of being a bear just now.' He handed her the glass, put his arm round her shoulders and gave her a quick hug.

Emma had to stop the wine splashing over her fingers and stared in surprise. She blustered. 'I didn't mean to sound grouchy either.'

Carmelita got up and said in a satisfied voice, 'If you two have forgiven one another, we can eat. The casserole is ready. I'll just check if the potatoes are done and finish off the salad.' Emma started to get up. Carmelita waved her back. 'Stay where you are, it's all organised! After I'd finished sorting him out, Damián helped.'

Damián and Pablo gave a belly laugh; clearly, it wasn't the first time Carmelita had given him a piece of her mind. Emma sank back into the chair, relieved that Pablo and Damián were soon talking in torrents of Spanish — probably about a successful strategy for tomorrow. She picked up a magazine from a side table and began to flip through the pages. His apology surprised her; it was totally unexpected. She reflected that he was very honest and didn't pussy-foot around. Even if he was sometimes almost too frank and straightforward, Emma preferred that. You knew where you stood.

Damián eventually finished fifth.

He always handled his own finances; with his brother's help. They got advice from an investment banker but Damián made his own decisions about what he did with his earnings. Emma's eyes boggled sometimes when she saw the sums involved. He invested most of his prize-money in land or property. She sometimes had to act as a go-between him and his brother, when Damián was busy on the golf course and she thought Julio sounded like an amiable and likeable person.

Emma and Damián never again mentioned the day they'd squabbled. Any further discussion would have been counter-productive. When Damián went out, Emma never asked him or the others where he was going, but he seemed to be making an effort to be discreet, because there was no bad publicity. Emma sometimes went to the cinema with Carmelita, or with Pablo and Carmelita for a meal, if Damián was out. Making friendships was difficult — they were never in one place long enough. Carmelita knew a lot of people on the world circuit, and if they used the car and picked up Damián and Pablo after the game, they were soon in the centre of a crowd in the clubhouse bar. Some of the younger players eyed Emma speculatively and she just hoped she hadn't been branded as Damián's mistress.

Gradually her efforts began to pay off. Most newspaper reports these days were concerned with his performance on the golf course. Emma was pleased. If he was meeting girls, he kept it quiet. Outwardly, she pretended she didn't care, but inside she didn't want to think about him having an affair. She experienced a gamut of perplexing emotions about Damián Alvarez. Emma was glad they were always on the move; it left her less time for worrying about her reactions.

* * *

The next tournament wasn't a top event, but a large number of visitors came every day to see a top player. Damián enjoyed the attention. He gave an interview on the final day, and Emma felt unnecessarily resentful when she watched the polished way he handled the attractive blond TV reporter who was blatantly flirting with him.

He won the competition, and donated a cup for the 'Best Up-and-coming Player of the Year' and hoped to be invited back next year. That produced a round of rousing applause. Emma had made a long trip the previous day to find a suitable trophy.

After dinner, before they all went to pack, they were still lingering around the polished table in the dining room. Cradling the glass with the last of her dry white wine, Emma tilted her head and said to Damián. 'You seem to enjoy small tournaments almost more than the big ones.'

Through the French windows, the sun was fading from a sky drained of colour, and only one bright star was swimming in a sea of black velvet. The wind was fresh and it fretted impatiently at the shutters. The smell of old-fashioned roses on the sideboard fought with the fading smell of freshly ground coffee and ripe strawberries.

The beginning of a smile tipped the

corner of Damián's mouth. 'Yes, you're probably right. There are thousands of less-prestigious tournaments like this. They're testing grounds for talented youngsters. That's why I wanted to donate a cup as well as money today. Having your name on a challenge cup is proof that you're going places.' He leaned forward, picked up his glass and tossed the remains down in one gulp. Settling back, he flexed his shoulders and his shirt strained dangerously. He smiled at her and she felt a glow. He looked at his watch. 'It's been a long day. I'm off!'

Emma couldn't decide whether he was more attractive in a dinner suit, or in denim stretch jeans and a striped sweatshirt. It didn't seem to make much difference what he wore — he always looked good. Emma was astonished at the sense of fulfilment she had at being part of this troupe. A short time ago, she didn't know they existed, and now she was fully integrated. Damián radiated a vitality that drew her to him like a magnet. She could understand why women buzzed around like bees around a honey pot. Being honest, she realised he was the kind of man who automatically wakened romantic notions in the women he met. She remembered how dissatisfied she'd been before she left the library, and how happy she was now. Sometimes Emma felt like a gipsy, always on the move, forever adapting to new surroundings and new circumstances.

5

Damián arrived home out of the blue one afternoon. Emma told herself that her heart was only pounding because of suddenly seeing a strange figure, then recognising it was him. She'd come in from the garden and was glad her eyes were hidden behind sunglasses. Her mind told her body not to feel so happy, but it refused to listen. 'You're on time! How did it go?'

He folded himself into a chair. 'Good, we were level at the end. See how it goes tomorrow.' He glanced around. 'This is a comfortable 'lived-in' kind of house. I like it.'

Emma took in the mottled crimson chairs, the long windows with their chorus of cream curtains and the stone flagged floor covered haphazardly with Persian carpets. 'Yes, it's restful and cosy, with lots of style, isn't it?'

'I'm longing for a shower, but I want to sort something out.'

Emma waited. She was used to him suddenly talking business when she least expected. 'I looked at our schedule last night; there are a couple of days between the end of this one and the tournament in South Africa.'

Emma nodded. 'Yes, do you want to go straight to Johannesburg.'

'No; book us back to Barcelona. Pablo needs some Spanish air, and Carmelita is dying to catch up on family gossip. If we leave after the final day here, we'll have almost a week.'

She nodded. 'I'll sort the tickets out. Where do you want to stay?'

'I'll phone Julio; he'll fix it. Just organise the flight tickets, non stop.'

'I don't think that's feasible. We'll probably have to fly via Heathrow.' Her thoughts brightened. 'I could leave you there, and we'd meet up later again.' Emma took off her sunglasses; she now felt strong enough to meet his eyes.

Resting his elbows on his knees, he

shook his head. 'I'd like you to come for a couple of days; to get a better insight into the financial side of things. It'd make your job easier.' He paused.

'I appreciate that you want to see parents and friends, but if you go home three or four days later, you still have plenty of time before we leave again.'

Emma avoided his glance and looked down. 'This is a personal visit, and I might be in the way . . .'

He rose smoothly. 'Pablo and Carmelita nearly always come for a day or two before taking off to their vineyard. You're one of us now!' He got up; clearly satisfied he'd settled everything and headed for the stairs.

Emma was slightly annoyed to find she was breathless, and had to admit it was getting harder to remain indifferent. The realisation unnerved her, but she told herself she'd soon get over such ridiculous emotions. She was most likely suffering from a kind of teenage idolatry, only in her case the idol was a sportsman. She refused to be sidetracked by romantic emotions about a man who didn't know what the word love meant!

★ ★ ★

On arrival in Spain,. Damián's brother met them. Julio and Damián clasped hands, and enveloped each other in bear-like hugs. Julio looked like Damián; he was younger, a few centimetres shorter, his face was squarer and more solid, but his eyes were the same inky black. Julio also knew Pablo and Carmelita, so the meeting was hearty and loud. Julio turned towards Emma, standing a little to the side, feeling nervous.

He clasped her by the shoulders, held her away to study her face. 'And this is Emma? We've spoken so often on the phone. You have a lovely voice, and your face is lovelier.' He leaned forward and kissed her cheek. 'Welcome to Spain, I hope you enjoy your stay.'

Emma coloured. 'Thanks, that's very kind. I'm sure I will!'

Damián's voice drifted over her shoulder. 'Stop flirting, or I'll tell your wife!'

Julio laughed and his eyes twinkled. 'Go ahead! She trusts me! If everyone's ready, follow me! The van's parked directly opposite. Is this all the luggage?' He led the way and they trailed after him, pushing trolleys loaded with luggage.

Emma looked forward to seeing the Spanish countryside. She didn't ask where they were going and she didn't really care. It was nice not to have any responsibilities. They got in a mini-bus. Pablo and Damián packed the suitcases in the back. Julio got in behind the wheel and Damián the passenger seat next to him. Pablo claimed the seat directly behind them, leaving Emma and Carmelita a free choice of the remaining five seats. Julio joined the stream of vehicles leaving the airport and they were soon on a main road leading south.

Damián started chatting to Julio in

Spanish. Their conversation was dotted with laughter. Pablo and Carmelita added comments now and then. If she stayed with them for any length of time, she'd have to make an effort and learn Spanish. She made herself comfortable, stretched her legs and leaned back. She didn't like all of what she saw along the way; lots of land was covered in ugly plastic; it looked like something out of a science-fiction movie.

The van purred and there was soft music playing. Emma relaxed. Some of the small villages often had quaint market squares and she wished they could stop and explore. Time passed quickly, and they turned in at a large sign announcing *La Calleja D'or — Golf de Cataluna,* and continued down the gravelled driveway towards a beautifully situated large hotel bathed in the last delightful rays of the afternoon sun.

Emma murmured, 'A golf hotel? I should've guessed!'

Damián looked back. 'Julio and I

own this place, where else would I stay?'

Emma's eyes widened. She looked out of the window. 'Good heavens!'

Damián said, 'It's one of Europe's best golf courses with a five star hotel, and all the facilities.'

Emma addressed Julio. 'And you run it?'

Julio laughed softly. 'Not on my own — but I keep the wheels turning. The hotel gives a lot of local people work and we attract visitors all through the year because of the mild climate.'

Emma looked around ahead with growing interest. 'It looks beautiful.'

Emma threw open the French windows. The bungalows were on a slope, overlooking the hotel. She stepped outside and gazed at the view. There was the sweep of a bay not far away. 'We're close to the sea?'

'Yes, a ten-minute walk across the grounds.' Damián joined her, his hands in his pockets. They stood in silence side by side for a moment.

The bungalows were identical. She indicated the small swimming pool, slap bang in the middle. 'What luxury — a private pool!'

'The bungalows were built for family and friends. Julio only ever rents them out if he's absolutely desperate! This is a home from home for me. Mine is directly opposite. Pablo and Carmelita are over there, and my parent's unit is on you right! The golf course is behind us.'

Emma didn't comment; she turned to face him. 'And where does Julio live?'

'Not far from here; but far enough to give him privacy.'

'Ummm! I expect he's glad to get away sometimes.' She slipped out of her sandals and lifted her skirt as she stepped down the first two shallow steps into the turquoise waters of the pool. It felt wonderful.

Damián watched her with amused expression. 'You'd like to have a quick swim or a shower? Help yourself! I'll be back in two hours to take you to dinner.'

Emma noted he'd mentioned his parents without visible resentment, so things weren't completely on the rocks. 'Right!' Emma smiled. He left and walked around the pool towards his bungalow. Emma could tell he was satisfied, but who wouldn't be — if you were part-owner of this place.

She went inside, explored the elegant small sitting room and stylish bedroom, and continued into the en-suite bathroom. She scanned the marble surfaces and the expensive fittings. With childish delight, she found soaps, shampoos, complimentary toothbrushes, toothpaste and a plentiful supply of luxurious thick, fluffy white towels. Nothing had been forgotten to make someone's stay something to remember. Just as she was hanging up her skirt, someone knocked. She put it back on, buttoning the waistband on the way to the door.

A smiling waiter in a short white jacket and black bow-tie was carrying a tray with a single long stemmed champagne glass, an iced bottle of champagne and a crystal bowl of white roses. *With the compliments of Senor Damián Alvarez.*

More than surprised, Emma thanked him, and took the tray.

Emma wondered why an employer should indulge his employee with champagne, flowers and a stay at a luxury hotel; she couldn't, and decided to revel in luxury and not speculate. With effort, she removed the wiring, extracted the cork, and filled her glass. The pale liquid fizzed and the bubbles rose in a never ending string as she lifted it to her lips. Delicious! She took the bowl of tightly budded roses, buried her face in them for a moment and inhaled the sweet perfume before placing them on the bedside table.

Taking another sip from her glass, she decided it would be sensible to have a shower before she got drunk. Drinking champagne on an empty stomach was full of hidden dangers!

Feeling pampered, she put on a short black linen dress that made her skin look like alabaster and pinned her hair back behind her ears with two large combs. Her hair tumbling to her shoulders was full of chestnut flames as it bounced. She took care not to overdo her make-up. Her brown eyes looked large in her pale face. She studied her reflection and was satisfied. Emma looked at her watch, and decided to enjoy a second glass.

Her mind revolved around a telephone conversation she'd had with her mother two days ago, when Emma explained she was visiting Spain first, before returning home.

Her mother's voice was full of worry, 'I don't like the sound of it! Normally secretaries don't need to be included in all of their employer's plans.'

'Oh Mum! We're more like a substitute family than his personal staff; and I'm the jack-of-all-trades. Damián wants me to get a better insight into his finances. Don't worry! Everything is fine, and I know what I'm doing.'

'Has he been in the headlines since

you got this job? Perhaps the British press hasn't picked it up. I check the sport-pages these days, as well as the gossip columns; and I'm not even interested in sport! I don't want you to get hurt. I know you're not stupid, and you're old enough to take care of yourself, but you could get dazzled and overwhelmed by the glamour. He's a celebrity — but with a reputation for loving and leaving wherever he goes.'

Emma knew her mother was only being sensible. 'He isn't as bad as the newspapers make him out to be.' She ignored the memory of the nightclub episode in the States and continued, 'He hasn't made a wrong move. I'm sure you'd like him, if you met him. He's very amiable and polite; there's not an ounce of snobbishness in him. Pablo tells me that lots of golfers get arrogant when they're rich and famous.'

'That applies to lots of other people, not just golfers! Perhaps I'm just biased, but what else can you expect, when you see what's written in the newspapers?'

Returning to the present, Emma looked at the dark green bottle with its imposing label. It was a shame that she wouldn't finish it; she was already tired and looking forward to bed. Tomorrow it would be flat and taste insipid.

Someone knocked on the door. She opened it and despite the fact that she should be used to seeing him, the breath caught in her throat as she looked up at Damián. His glance took in her dress and his eyes sparkled in the darkness. He smiled. 'Wow! I must say I have a very attractive assistant. Ready?'

Delighted by the compliment and with a half-filled glass in her hand, she lifted it and said, 'More or less! Thanks for this, and the flowers! The champagne tastes wonderful. I'm on my second glass!'

He lifted his black brows and looked amused. 'I thought a whole bottle was excessive, knowing you never drink a lot, but a half-bottle would have looked mean!' He tilted his head to the side and even though his face was in the half-shadow Emma's heart still managed to skip a beat. 'If you provide me with a tumbler, I'll share a glass.' He looked briefly at his watch. 'We still have time. A quarter of an hour on the terrace with a glass of champagne, before I face the family, is an excellent idea.'

Emma gestured him in. She picked up the heavy-glass bottle from the nearby table and handed to him. 'I'll get the glass.'

Damián went to sit outside. His legs were stretched out in front of him in a straight line. She asked, 'Sure you don't mind? It seems heathenish to drink champagne out of an ordinary tumbler.'

He shook his head and filled the glass. 'It's what's in the glass that matters, not what it looks like!' He lifted his glass in her direction. 'Cheers!'

Emma slipped gently into the chair

opposite, took a sip and then played absentmindedly with the stem of the glass. It was a peaceful evening and this was a quiet interlude, in a day of travel and settling in. Their conversation was full of easy silences between moments when he described how the hotel had been built and his links locally.

Emma stored the information. Soft sounds from the main hotel down below drifted towards them. Damián enjoyed the natural knack Emma had to bring tranquillity into his life, and he also liked her quick sense of humour. They were now so familiar with each other there was no need to perform; they were completely at ease.

In a pale blue shirt and light beige chinos, he looked young and very relaxed. Emma knew the emotions she felt were danger signals, but she was sure she had it all under control.

He leaned forward and looked at his watch; some stray moonbeams caught the metal frame. 'I wouldn't mind sitting here until bedtime, but if we don't join them soon, someone will come to fetch us.' He got up and held out his hand. She took it and faced him. They walked down the pathway leading from the bungalows. Shadows were creeping up the slope and they were alone with the darkness. Emma listened to the sound of gravel under their feet as they went side by side. She had the feeling they were alone in the world. The sensation didn't last long; soon they'd reached the hotel.

They walked towards a round table in the restaurant where Pablo, Carmelita and a middle aged couple were waiting. 'Mama this is Emma McKay. She organises my life for me.'

Emma held out her hand to the fine boned woman who studied her for a second or two. Emma noticed it was an expression that bordered on relief. Emma wondered if she'd been expecting a playgirl. Mrs Alvarez was wearing black silk trousers and a cream shirt with a long rope of pearls round her neck. She had a well-kept figure, smooth olive skin, and dark hair with strands of grey drawn back into an elegant chignon. The older woman took Emma's hand. 'I'm pleased to meet you, Emma. This is my husband, Juan.'

Emma turned to the man at her side and saw how Damián would look in thirty year's time. Pushing back his chair, he got up and held her hand for a moment. 'Welcome, my dear. Do you like Spain? Have you been here before?'

Emma replied. 'Once, but a long time ago! On the whole, I enjoyed myself.'

He nodded. 'Julio and Maria will be here soon; they're putting the children to bed and giving the babysitter last minute instructions.' He smiled.

Carmelita patted the empty chair at her side. 'Come here, Emma.'

Emma complied gratefully. Her notion that Damián's parents were simple farm people went by the board. They might not be rolling in money, but they weren't hard-up either. Watching them and listening to Carmelita's chatter, she remembered Pablo's account about

Damián and his parents and their row. She saw they were polite to each other, but there was a barrier — two miles high and five miles round. She shook out the white serviette and laid it across her lap.

It was an enjoyable meal. When Julio arrived with his wife, Emma found she was petite, pretty with dark curly hair and friendly grey eyes. They all made an effort to bring Emma into the conversation. She caught Damián's eye across the table and he gave her a questioning look. She smiled, so he was free to busy himself with his sister-in-law. She decided to leave early to give the family time together. They were all still drinking coffee and brandy when she got up, and said goodnight. Carmelita and Pablo joined her and they wandered back arm in arm to the bungalows.

Drawing the curtains across the French windows before she went to bed, she noticed there was still no light in Damián's bungalow.

6

Next morning Emma woke as sun-beams were stealing around the edge of the curtains. She dressed in cotton trousers, a T-shirt, and a lacy cardigan in shades of green. In the restaurant there were no familiar faces, in fact it was practically empty. There was smell of breakfast in the air. She read an English newspaper while enjoying the food. Pablo and Carmelita arrived just as she was about to leave. The restaurant was busier now. Carmelita beamed as she sat down. She looked around with appreciation. Emma finished her coffee, folded her serviette and stood up. 'I'm going for a walk to get rid of the cobwebs!'

Carmelita looked startled and looked around. 'Cobwebs?'

Emma tried to explain. 'People say that when they're still half-asleep!'

'Oh, I see — get rid of cobwebs . . . good!' Carmelita nodded. 'Why don't you go to the beach?'

'That's a good idea!'

Pablo looked out of the panorama windows and shook his head. 'Don't stay long. The wind is moving fast and rain clouds on the horizon.'

Emma wondered how he knew. There was no sun, but no clouds either. Carmelita looked at Pablo and gave Emma a knowing smile. Emma left them and walked along a path in the direction of the bay. There was a fresh breeze, but it wasn't unpleasant. Emma passed some gardeners; they smiled and greeted her politely in Spanish. She saw there were already people out on the golf course in the distance.

The path petered out at the cliff edge and she found the steps down to the beach. Someone was on the sand at the far end of the cove. Emma descended quickly, pulled her cardigan tighter around her slight form and walked towards the water. She loved the wind and the salty air and when she reached the water's edge, she took off her sandals. The water was cold. Emma stood in pleasure for a while and then decided to walk as far as the end of the small cove. A friendly Labrador bounded towards her. Emma came abreast of its owner. The man was sun-beaten and wrinkled. He lifted his straw hat in a gesture of old fashioned politeness and pointed with his silver topped cane towards the sky above them.

'I think we're in for a downpour.'

Emma smiled at him and looked up to where the clouds were steely grey and moving fast. 'I'm just going to the end of the bay.'

His eyes twinkled. 'It's further than you think!' Donning his hat again, he fought his way against the wind towards the steps.

After walking briskly for several minutes, Emma felt the first raindrop. There was nowhere to shelter so she ran back towards the steps. It poured down in a grey sheet before she reached them. Soon, her hair hung in rats-tails and her clothes clung uncomfortably to her body. Up on top, she sheltered under a tree with thick foliage until the rain finally stopped.

On the way back to the bungalows, she rubbed her hair with a damp kerchief and fluffed it up in a hopeless attempt to give it shape. She stopped in her tracks when she came round the corner and saw Damián talking to a tall elegant woman. They were standing close together outside his bungalow; he had his hands in his pockets and they seemed to be having an animated conversation. Emma viewed them for a few seconds; she didn't want to interrupt and decided to slip away to the cloakroom in the hotel to find a towel. She turned on her heels. The movement caught his eye and he beckoned to her.

'Ah, Emma! Come here. I'd like you to meet a friend of mine. This is Elena, Senora Elena Mendez . . . Elena, this is

Emma — Emma McKay.'

Emma had no choice but to join them. She held out her hand and plastered a stiff smile across her face. 'Hello! I'm pleased to meet you!'

The dark haired woman studied Emma, and took her hand; she smiled briefly. 'Hello!' The smile didn't quite reach her eyes.

She was tall, almost on eye-level with Damián. She had flashing, almond-shaped black eyes, and a smooth olive complexion. The beautifully cut thick black hair flowed in waves around her chin. With a thin nose, high cheek-bones, the figure of a top-model, and beautiful features, she was a striking woman by anyone's standards. So, this was Damián's ex-girlfriend? A knot formed in Emma's throat and she drew her arms around herself and tried to think of something sensible to say. She was glad when Damián saved her the effort.

'Elena plays golf; she wants me to give her tips on how to improve her game.' Emma nodded mutely.

Elena touched him and the red-tipped fingers slid down his muscled arms in a kind of possessive gesture. He didn't move, and didn't respond. Elena smiled at him, and hardly gave Emma a glance. 'If Damián can't help me, then no one can.' With a throaty laugh, she added conspiratorially. 'My husband is a keen golfer, and I'd like to outshine him.' She didn't expect a comment from Emma; her smile was only for Damián.

Damián's expression was unreadable. 'The resident instructor knows this course like the back of his hand. You'd learn more from him than from me. My teaching skills are rusty.'

'That wouldn't be so much fun!' Elena waited and when no reply came, she turned to Emma. 'I suppose you're an excellent golfer?'

Damián tipped his head back and gave a gruff laugh. His black eyebrows lifted and his eyes twinkled when he said. 'Emma? Emma doesn't know a putter from an iron. She's not interested.'

Elena's eyebrows lifted. She looked at Damián and smiled. 'Really? How strange!' She tucked her arm through Damián's. 'Any woman ought to be interested in everything you do!'

Tongue in cheek Damián asked, 'What do you say to that, Emma?'

Defiantly Emma straightened her shoulders. 'Of course I'm interested in my boss — he pays my wages, but I don't have to play golf. My job is to see he can concentrate on the game.' Her colour heightened.

Elena's face showed slight irritation; she licked her scarlet lips. 'I see and understand now! Anyone who leads a busy life needs staff to keep things running smoothly. I couldn't cope if my own servants didn't run my house so efficiently for me.'

Emma bristled, and her nails dug into the flesh of her palms. She didn't mind being branded as Damián's servant, but it didn't sit easily coming from Elena's lips.

The corner of Damián's mouth twitched; he looked into the distance. Elena directed another question at him. 'Is Emma . . . The name came out hesitatingly. 'Is Emma coming tonight?'

Emma looked at Damián and was puzzled. 'Tonight?'

He hastened to explain to Emma. 'I've arranged for us to see some flamenco, as I promised.' He answered Elena, 'Yes, Emma is coming.'

Emma didn't show she hadn't been asked. 'Oh, I'm looking forward to it.'

Elena threw back her head and laughed loudly. 'We're all looking forward to it; me especially.' Emma nodded silently; if Elena was going, the prospect wasn't very tempting any more.

She'd rather not watch Elena and Damián together, even if Elena was married to someone else.

To Emma's relief Carmelita and Pablo came round the corner. They nodded casually at Elena. Carmelita threw her arm around Emma's shoulders. 'Did you enjoy your . . . ?'

She stopped mid-sentence, and ran her hand down the girl's arm, touched Emma's hair and felt the shoulder of her dress. 'Emma! You're all wet through!'

Emma smiled weakly. 'I should have listened to Pablo, shouldn't I? I didn't really expect rain; it was so nice when I set out.'

Damián reached out and felt the arm of her cardigan. His lips stiffened. 'Instead of standing around being polite, you should have been getting out of those wet clothes long ago!'

Rattled by his tone, she answered sharply. 'I'm perfectly all right!' She conceded. 'I only need a hot shower! Excuse me!' Emma turned away and pulled the key out of her pocket. She was glad to leave the group. Emma was imagining Elena and Damián together when they were young and in love — full of plans for an exciting future together. Suddenly she felt extremely tired. Shedding her clothes on the bathroom floor, she stayed under the shower until the warmth returned to her body. Once her hair was dry, she felt a little better.

It was quiet outside again; everyone had disappeared. Emma carried her book out onto the terrace. Damián and Elena were probably out on the golf-course together by now. Emma wondered if Elena's husband cared? She had a headache and wasn't hungry, so she decided to give lunch a miss. Pulling the bedcover up to her chin, she fell into a fitful sleep.

It was mid-afternoon when she woke. She hoped her tiredness was due to the lack of fresh air and went for a walk. She didn't enjoy it, and noticed she had a sore-throat as well as a bad headache. She'd listen to Pablo next time! She watched the news on satellite TV and looked at her wristwatch. Her headache and sore throat were getting worse, so she decided it was sensible to give the evening meal, and the flamenco outing, a miss. She went across to tell Carmelita, went to bed early and spent a restless night sipping iced water in the hope of relieving her sore throat.

★ ★ ★

Next morning she felt even worse. Her face felt hot but her body was cold, and she had spells of shivering. Feeling pretty miserable, she decided to stay in bed. Knocking at the door finally brought her to her feet. It was Carmelita. Carmelita took one look and said. 'We wondered where you were. But it's obvious — can I get you something?'

Emma pushed the hair out of her flushed face, and tried to smile. 'I'd love some orange juice and something to treat a sore throat if you can find anything.'

Carmelita put her hand on Emma's forehead. 'Ummm . . . temperature too, I think. Get back into bed. I'll see what I can do.' Emma was glad to comply.

Carmelita called back over her shoulder. 'Leave the door open, I'll be back.'

Emma was dozing and imagined something like a gentle kiss across her forehead before she opened her eyes and felt a cool hand. She was expecting Carmelita and bewildered to find Damián. She was already flushed with a slight temperature but her colour heightened when she found him peering at her.

Emma tried to push herself upright, and with a voice that sounded very strange and croaked badly she said, 'Damián! What are you doing here?'

His hands pushed her down again. He looked uneasy. 'I came to see for myself.' Sitting next to her on the bed, he announced, 'I'm sending for the doctor.' He knew her protest would come, and choked it in the bud. 'No arguments! I'm responsible for your well-being. It's up to me not you!'

Emma's heart lurched madly She pushed the reddish-brown curls back from her ears. It was completely irrelevant, but she wondered how humdrum she must look in his eyes. Her sensible Marks & Spencer cotton pyjamas must be quite a contrast to the satin and silk he usually viewed. Ah well! She tried to clear her throat and sound normal but her words were scratchy and slurred when she spoke. 'It's only a cold, Damián. Don't fuss!'

He got up, and the mattress righted itself again. He viewed her with a touch of concern. 'I'm not fussing. You've a temperature, your throat is all to pot, and you feel terrible otherwise you wouldn't be lying in bed. The hotel has an agreement with a local doctor; he comes whenever a guest is ill. I'll send for him, and when he gets here, Carmelita will bring him over. She said you wanted some orange juice; I'll fetch a glass.' He fetched a tumbler from the bathroom and put it on the bedside-table next to the juice and roses. He turned towards the door.

Emma sat up and croaked. 'How was the flamenco evening?

He paused at the door and nodded, 'Yes, it was good and a pity that you missed it.' He gripped the doorframe and gave her a smile. 'I hope you'll soon feel better. Do as the doctor says — no rebellion!'

In a rough voice, she answered. 'As if I was ever rebellious!' Emma pulled out a pillow from behind her back and threw it at him; it missed its mark.

With sympathetic eyes, he lifted his hand and closed the door quietly.

After a couple of doses of medication, she began to feel a lot better and slept peacefully. Carmelita called later and mentioned Damián and Julio were leaving to meet a banker in Barcelona, and would be gone all day. Emma had a bad conscience, this was why she'd come to Spain. She comforted herself; she wasn't much use to anyone at present. She spent the day in bed and was lively enough to watch TV in the evening. She also managed some soup she ordered via room-service.

Next morning she no longer had a

temperature so she got up, had a shower and dressed. Her nose was running and the cold was still hanging on, but things were improving fast. She was also hungry. Her flight home was booked for later that afternoon, so she'd have to pack after breakfast. Carmelita called on her way to breakfast; Pablo was with her.

Emma could smile again. 'I'm hungry!'

'And you look a lot better! Why don't you have breakfast on the terrace? Order what you fancy!'

Emma looked hesitant.

'Oh Emma! Spoil yourself and save your energy!'

Emma thought about her trip home that afternoon. 'Oh, all right, I will! Thanks for all your help Carmelita.'

Carmelita smiled gratefully and Pablo ruffled her hair before they both left.

The omelette, orange juice, coffee, toast and marmalade tasted wonderful. Out on the small terrace, the morning air was laden with herbs and salt from the sea. Even though her nose wasn't completely unblocked, she still managed to pick out some of the smells around her. Her heart skipped when she saw Damián step out of the French windows and come across. He threw himself into the neighbouring chair, and viewed her critically.

'You look so much better.'

'Yes, I feel a lot better, too.'

'No temperature?'

'No, the doctor left a thermometer for me to check.' She looked across. 'Carmelita told me you went to see your banker yesterday. I'm sorry I wasn't with you; that was the whole point of my coming here, wasn't it?'

He shook his head. 'Don't give it another thought. Julio and I went over everything, and I'll tell you what you need to know. It's mainly about transferring money, and where you can get large amounts of cash quickly, if I need it.'

'I've a bad conscience.'

'There's no need!' He gave her a

smile that sent her pulses racing. 'How about a walk? It'll do us both good.'

It was hard to remain indifferent; her resistance levels were low. 'I'd like to, but I must pack. My flight leaves at four this afternoon.'

He waved his hand offhandedly. 'Oh, forget that! I cancelled it two days ago.'

Her eyes widened and she stared at him. 'You did what? I want to see my parents before we leave for South Africa! I promised my mother I'd see her.' She thought ahead. 'Even if I get a flight tomorrow, I'll only have one evening at home before we leave on Saturday!'

He leaned back and locked his hands behind his head. The chair creaked softly under his weight. 'I talked to Pablo, and we decided it wasn't a good idea for you and Carmelita to come to Johannesburg. There's too much street violence, and we can't keep an eye on you all the time. We decided to book into a hotel on the course — and we were lucky, they made room for us at short notice even though they're officially booked out. We'll manage without you for once. It gives you more time to throw off your cold and Carmelita will enjoy some extra time in Spain. You, Pablo and me, travel to London on Saturday. We'll leave you there, and we'll be back for a two day break before we meet up again for the flight on the 20th.

'Have you already booked everything for our first stop in Australia?'

Emma's mouth was slightly open. 'Yes. You've re-organised things without telling me?'

His eyes were hooded. 'Why not? I'm still capable of organising my schedules, Emma. I haven't forgotten how! I thought you'd be pleased to have a week at home with your family and friends.'

Emma looked down. 'Yes, yes of course I am. I'm surprised that's all. I'll have to warn my parents.' She put her hands on the arms of the chair.

'I've already done that. I've spoken to

your mother and explained all about the changes to our plans.'

Emma's eyes grew wide and her brows were raised in question. 'You've spoken to my mother?'

With an expression of satisfaction, he said, 'Naturally! I realised she'd worry if you didn't turn up today. She agreed with me when I said you should cure your cold before you come home. She sounds a very charming and sensible woman.'

Emma drew a deep breath. Obviously, her mother had been so overwhelmed that she didn't have time to ask any probing questions, or make awkward comments. Damián had turned on the full force of his charm and won her over.

'Finish your coffee and wrap up!' He got up. 'I'm going to get myself a pullover; back in five minutes. We'll take a leisurely stroll for as long as you like. I've promised to play golf with Elena and her husband this afternoon, but I hope that you'll have dinner in the restaurant this evening,'

She was appreciative of the fact that he'd thought far enough to inform her parents about the change of plans. 'I'd enjoy a walk and I'm definitely eating in the restaurant tonight.'

He smiled. 'Good! Pity that you missed the flamenco, but there'll be other opportunities. Pablo and Carmelita are going home this afternoon, my parents are leaving after dinner, and the Mendezes are leaving this afternoon too, so it'll be a lot quieter around here for the last day or so.'

'That means there's only you, me and your parents for dinner tonight?'

He nodded.

Emma decided that things were getting more complicated with every passing day. Was her feeling pure infatuation, or had it tunnelled itself much, much, deeper. She picked up her cup and watched him as he strolled back to his bungalow. His hand was on the door when Elena came round the corner. Emma noticed his polite smile, and they talked for a few minutes.

Elena looked across and made a rippling movement with her fingers. Emma waved back, and noted how Elena placed her long red-tipped fingers on his arm again. Emma got up abruptly and went indoors.

Later, when she walked with Damián, she buried her irritation at seeing him and Elena together. They walked aimlessly. Continual conversation wasn't necessary. It was enough to amble in companionable silence, or just talk about anything that came to mind. Emma could tell he felt contented; she could sense when something bothered him. She made no demands on him, and he seemed to enjoy her company. Emma loved the way his comments followed unusual and attention-grabbing trails. For someone who said he didn't have enough time to read informative books or newspapers, he possessed a wealth of information and he had an intelligent brain. He had an intriguing way of seeing things.

With his hands thrust deep in the pocket of his soft leather jacket, and hair ruffled untidily by gentle breezes, he looked carefree and contented. 'Sure you're warm enough?'

Emma smiled and nodded. 'This fresh air and this place is just what I need.'

'Even though it's partly mine, I must say it's nice here, isn't it? In fact I could imagine living close to somewhere like this when I give up golfing.'

'Not long ago you said you intended to go on as long as you enjoyed it!'

'I will, but I won't be able to travel the top circuits forever. Somewhere like this with a house nearby would be ideal. I could golf every day for my own pleasure, and perhaps I could coach up and coming talents. I like being with youngsters, do you?'

Emma hadn't thought about it much before. She considered briefly and answered. 'Yes, I suppose I do. Having children is probably lots of fun, and lots of work!' Emma remembered that

Spanish people were usually very fond of children. She imagined Damián with children — probably he'd get on like a house on fire, because he was very honest and very impulsive. With a lump in her throat, she realised she loved the idea of Damián with children very much.

He added, 'I'd like to be around to watch my kids grow up; and I'd like to have time to make real friendships, outside the world of golfing.'

Emma was silent for a moment. 'If that's what you want, you'll get it. You're a very determined character. Finding a wife will be the least of your problems; they're probably already forming an orderly queue.' She gave him a happy smile, and he grinned back. 'And you make friends easily, so I don't think that'll be a problem either. You'll settle down easily when you put your mind to it.'

He stopped walking and stared into the distance for a moment. 'Money can't buy everything. You need the right partner otherwise none of that will work.'

Without further comment, they headed back towards the bungalows again.

7

Instead of flying, Emma had an afternoon nap, slept deeply, and woke feeling
hungry. It was early, and there were still
a few hours until the evening meal, so
she picked up her book and a bowl of
grapes and went to enjoy the last rays of
sunshine. The small terrace was protected from the wind by partitions. She
looked across the turquoise water of the
swimming pool, and regretted that she
hadn't used it. A shadow fell across her
book; she looked up to find Damián's
mother standing there.

'Hello! Are you feeling better?'

'Thanks, yes — much better!'

'May I join you?'

Emma indicated the empty chair.
'Please! Make yourself comfortable.'

The older woman crossed her legs
and smiled at Emma. 'Tell me about
yourself; we haven't had a chance to

talk. Where did you meet Damián?'

Emma told her. His mother's mouth curved and she commented. 'Hmmm! He's lucky that you wanted to work for him after that.'

Emma shrugged philosophically. 'I don't think he's the womaniser and adventurer the press make him out to be. He's attractive, a celebrity, and he's well-off. He's a perfect target for gossip columnists. I don't understand why they don't accept he's entitled to live his life as he likes.'

'What do your parents think about you working for him?'

'They were very sceptical, but I think they've accepted things now. I think they thought he was looking for another scalp for his belt!' Mrs Alvarez looked puzzled so Emma added quickly as an explanation. ' . . . another easy conquest!'

She laughed. 'I find it hard to understand — all the admiration and publicity, but I understand your parents. All parents worry constantly about their children, however old they are. To be honest, I wondered what kind of woman you were, but you get on well with him . . . in a perfectly normal friendly way.'

'I think he finds it's a novelty not to have a fawning female grovelling at his feet.' Emma's voice was full of laughter and his mother's mouth twitched with amusement as Emma continued. 'Your son is a thoroughly nice and intelligent person despite what the newspapers report. I enjoy working for him.'

Mrs Alvarez studied the young woman opposite and liked her; she was an attractive young woman with lots of common sense and she understood Damián. 'I'm glad.'

Emma asked, 'Would you like something to drink?'

His mother shook her head. 'No, thank you!' She leaned forward and her expression steadied. 'His father and I underestimated Damián's determination to make a career out of golfing. We tried to stop him. We'd like to put things right, but it gets more difficult all the time.'

Emma took a deep breath. 'Why not just do whatever you think it will take?'

Mrs Alvarez smiled nervously. 'We keep waiting for the right moment.'

'Is there ever a right moment? Just let him know you realise things went well off-track for a while and that you're sorry.'

She stared into the distance. 'We thought golf was just a passing obsession back in those days. He'd just broken up with Elena. You know about Elena?'

Emma tried to look unconcerned and merely nodded.

'We thought that was the real reason why he went away, but when he became increasingly successful, we realised golf wasn't a passing fad and that he was very talented. We seldom saw him afterwards, and we've never had the courage to admit we were wrong.'

'His family means a lot to him, even

though he doesn't show it. Damián wants things to be right.'

Mrs Alvarez nodded and took a handkerchief out of her trouser pocket. She blew her nose. 'You're right — it's never too late, is it?' She straightened her shoulder and looked pointedly at Emma's book. 'What are you reading?'

Emma welcomed the change of subject. 'It's called *The Shadow of the Wind* by a Spanish author. I expect you know it?'

'Yes, of course. I enjoyed it too, very much,' she said. 'Perhaps you'll speak Spanish yourself one day, then you'll be able to read Spanish books in their original language.'

'I probably won't be with Damián long enough.'

'Oh, I do hope so! Damián seems more relaxed than when we saw him last time. You're the only big difference, so it must have something to do with you . . .'

Emma eyed her and didn't say what she thought; perhaps it was Elena's reappearance that was causing the change.

' . . . I'm glad that you're with him.'

The next couple of days were great. Damián played golf, she read a couple of books, and they met for meals, drinks in the bar, and went for long walks together — with her arm often tucked comfortably in his. The prickle of excitement when they were linked fretted at her like a dizzying current of wind racing through her body. She was pleased about their familiarity, she drifted along when she was with him, and his nearness kindled feelings of fire and need.

Emma wondered how long she could possibly keep this up without doing, or saying, something very stupid.

They went out for a meal on the final evening, to a small Spanish restaurant not far from the hotel. She enjoyed it immensely. His face haunted her whether she was awake or asleep. Emma hadn't yet figured out how she was going to live without knowing he was somewhere nearby.

* * *

Emma enjoyed the week at home, even though she missed Damián. She tried hard to concentrate on other things and reminded herself this was what life would be like when she returned to normality. She visited her parents, went on a shopping spree, and met some friends, but even though she tried to ignore thoughts of Damián, he continued to buzz around her brain. In two days time she was meeting them all at the airport again. She was sorting out clothes, and planned to spend a quiet evening at home. Tomorrow, she was taking her parents out for a meal.

Folding some soft pullovers, a sharp knock on the door startled her. Looking through the spy-hole, she was taken aback to see Robert standing there. Emma hadn't seen him since they'd broken up, and that was months, almost a lifetime, before she started working for Damián. She tried to inject enthusiasm into her voice. 'Robert!

What a surprise! How did you know I was home?'

As always, he was dressed impeccably in an Italian suit with matching shirt, and formal tie. His shoes shone and his hair was combed sleekly to one side. He was a successful banker and, for a while, his aura of perfection had impressed Emma a lot, until she found he was a window-dummy; immaculately groomed but with a lot of important things missing.

After they'd met a couple of times, he'd started talking about their future together. Emma had ignored it and didn't pay much attention; she was still hoping then he'd turn out to be Mr Right. He did have qualities that she appreciated, like reliability and dependability, but he was also very inflexible and always correct. He didn't make her feel that she was special.

She'd eventually come to the conclusion that a lifetime with Robert would be a nightmare. He'd started to include phrases like 'when we're engaged' or 'when we're married' in their conversations, and it was then Emma had decided it was time to end things. She'd done it as gently as she could. He'd been aggressively angry, insisting that she'd been unfair, that she'd wasted his precious time.

Emma had been mad; she'd never tried to mislead him about anything. She'd left him sitting in the same hotel where she'd met Damián, and hadn't seen or heard from him since then.

Emma wondered why he'd come. 'What can I do for you? How are things?'

Robert thrust a bunch of pink carnations at her as he came in. She closed the door, put the flowers on the dining table, and gestured towards the sofa.

Robert arranged himself, looking with disapproval at the pullovers. Automatically Emma picked them up, and took them to the adjoining room. Robert hadn't changed; a tidy sofa was paramount to Emma, or anything else.

She tried to be calm. 'Would you like a drink?'

'I'll have a whisky, if you have one.'

Emma poured some into a squat glass. Still curious and slightly flustered, she sat down and waited.

Robert took a sip and put it down on the table between them. He straightened his tie, and adjusted the sleeve of his jacket so that his shirt cuff peeped out. 'I've read that you're now working for Damián Alvarez.'

She was a little puzzled. 'What does that have to do with you?'

'I must admit I was shocked. The man has a dreadful reputation, and however much I don't understand why we didn't make it, that was still easier to accept than knowing you chose to work with someone like him, day in and day out — and all this travelling . . . '

Emma's hackles were rising. 'To be perfectly honest, it is none of your business what I do, or who my boss is. For your information Damián Alvarez is a perfect gentleman.'

'Huh! That's not what the newspapers say.'

'The newspapers quite often write a lot of drivel; you're foolish if you believe all they print about so-called celebrities.'

There were spots of bright colour on his cheeks. 'I didn't come here to argue with you about Damián Alvarez.'

She frowned in exasperation. 'Why did you come?'

He cleared his throat. 'I met your mother by chance and she said you were home for a couple of days. I thought I'd call, and tell you I've thought about why you didn't accept my proposal. Perhaps I forced things too fast at the time. I'm willing to overlook the last couple of months. My door is still open, Emma.'

She had to swallow hard. 'Pardon! What on earth are you talking about? I can't remember you proposing. You told me what I was going to do! You took everything for granted, as you always did. That's your trouble; you assume everyone is on the same wavelength. You don't leave anyone room to grow and to breathe.'

He looked unmoved. 'That's not true! Someone in a relationship has to channel things to a positive conclusion. I'm prepared to forget the past, and renew our relationship. I'll even forgive you this episode with Damián Alvarez, although I don't ever want to know what actually happened.' He leaned back with a smirk on his face.

She stood up and fixed her hands on her hips. 'Robert, let's get something straight. I don't need, or want, your forgiveness. I've no intention of renewing anything. We're finished. I haven't had a moment's regret that we broke up. I don't mind being friends, but I'll never feel anything more than friendship.'

He pursed his lips and his eyes narrowed. 'You don't mean that.'

Her mouth fell open, and she wondered how she could get him to leave. Another knock interrupted her thoughts and she threw the door open to find Damián standing there with a long-stemmed white rose. He offered it and she automatically accepted. 'A rose for a rose!' There was a quirk to his mouth.

Her heart plunged to her stomach and somersaulted back to hammer like mad against her ribs. He was tanned a deeper shade than when she'd last seen him and his eyes sparkled in the semi-darkness.

'Hi, Emma!'

'What . . . what are you doing here?'

'The tournament finished punctually, Pablo and I took the next flight out. I got in to London an hour ago; he's gone on to Barcelona. I wondered if you'd like to come for a meal?'

'A meal? A meal . . . now . . . with you?' Emma was struggling with her feelings

He looked amused. 'Yes. Are you suffering from deafness? A meal. You know, food and drink and all that.' He looked over her shoulder. 'Aren't you going to ask me in?'

'How did you know where I live?'

Smiling knowingly he explained. 'It's on a piece of paper you gave me once, and I double-checked with your mother!'

Emma was slightly breathless and lost for words; she stood aside. 'You'd better come in.'

He did, his expression steadied when he saw Robert. Soberly he said, 'Oh, am I butting in? Sorry, I didn't stop to think you might have a visitor.' He advanced and held out his hand. 'Damián Alvarez, how do you do?'

Robert accepted his hand gingerly and looked uncomfortable. Emma put the rose down and picked up the carnations. 'Robert was just about to leave. Thanks for calling Robert! I'm glad we've sorted things out.'

Damián lifted his hand. 'Please, don't leave because of me. I don't want to interrupt anything. I'll be seeing Emma soon anyway — in the course of business.'

Emma was so glad he was there, but couldn't say so. She marched to the door and opened it. 'All the best Robert! I hope you find what you're looking for.'

Robert got up hastily, brushed past Damián with heightened colour and grabbed the carnations as he went, without another word. Emma closed the door with unnecessary force.

Damián watched her carefully. 'What was that about?'

'Robert's an ex-boyfriend. He doesn't know when to take no for an answer.'

Damián looked more cheerful. 'Ah well! He has my sympathy! Love is a battlefield sometimes, isn't it?' He looked around the compact flat. 'So, this is your little nest? Nice!'

Emma looked at him suspiciously. 'Don't you try to be benevolent! I know I don't own anything comparable as even the cheapest of your possessions, but it is mine!' She added in more tranquilly. 'Even if I'm still paying it off! When it's mine, I'll be able to replace this jumble of furniture with some decent stuff and then it'll look really nice.'

He looked amused and held up his hands in a gesture of defence. 'Hey, Emma calm down! I like it! I wouldn't say so if it wasn't true. My first flat was a two-roomed one in the less popular area of Barcelona; I still have it. I swear your flat is much, much nicer!'

Emma tossed her head, pushed some hair back and nodded. 'I inherited some money from my grandparents, added my savings and borrowed the rest from my parents. I pay them back according to how I'm fixed. It's ideal for me because no bank can foreclose if I lose my job suddenly.'

He nodded. 'Sensible of you; and good of your parents!' He shifted his weight and tipped his head to the side. 'Well, do you want to come out for a meal or not?'

She answered in a more kindly tone. 'If you got in an hour ago, you're probably whacked. Would you rather I rustle something up for us here?'

Jauntily he cocked his dark head to one side. 'Don't tempt me!'

'Sit down! Or better still, open that bottle of wine on the cupboard first. I can only offer spaghetti with tomato sauce and salad — if you fancy anything else, we'll have to go out. My fridge is almost empty because of us leaving on Saturday.' She picked up the rose, shortened it and put it into a champagne flute in the middle of the table.

He divested himself of his coat and left it over the back of one of the chairs. He loosened his tie and came towards her. 'It sounds perfect!' Picking up the bottle opener and talking to her at the same time, he asked, 'Were you really thinking of marrying him?'

Clattering busily with saucepans, Emma answered. 'Robert? I couldn't make up my mind at first. He believed we were made for each other. Admittedly, I thought he was attractive, but when I got to know him better I found he was terribly pedantic. Everything has to be 100 per cent in his world. It's black, or white . . . nothing is grey. If you don't fit his ideas, he tries to make you fit. In the end, I was being smothered, and nothing I thought important meant much to him. He's good at his job, and has excellent prospects, but money isn't everything is it? Not when you're thinking about possibly spending the rest of your life with someone.'

Damián came to lean his hands on the working surface that topped some cupboards separating the kitchen section from the rest of the living room. 'No it's not! I knew you were intelligent. You clearly recognised that he's a stuffed shirt and full of his own importance, and I'm sure you would never have been happy with a man like him.'

She smiled at his wise words, and Damián smiled back.

She boiled water in the electric kettle to speed things up, poured it into a saucepan and dropped spaghetti into the salted liquid. 'Tell me about South Africa; how did it go?'

'I came in second! Missed it by a shot, but the whole thing could've gone either way. The prize money is still good. I'm going to win in Australia!'

Emma chuckled. 'Have you warned the others?'

'South Africa is beautiful.' He picked up a slice of cucumber from the chopping board, and started to nibble. 'My parents came to watch me.'

Emma's knife paused in mid-air for a moment. 'Really? Did they enjoy themselves? I get the impression that there's a bit of tension in the air. I don't understand it. Your mother seems nice; your father is more overwhelming, but I expect that wears off when you know him better.'

With an edge of reproach in his voice, he said, 'They were against me becoming a full time golfer ... but during dinner one evening my father admitted they hadn't realised how serious I'd been.' His expression was brighter. 'We pussy-footed around a bit but then it got easier and easier to talk about what happened.' His eyes twinkled brightly and added. 'Now I wish I knew how to avoid my mother's hugs and kisses! I think she's trying to make up for lost time; it's embarrassing!' He sucked the tip of his fingers as the rest of the cucumber disappeared into his mouth. 'We had a good time after that, and my father and I got tipsy once or twice.'

Emma nodded and sliced some tomatoes. 'Good! Families shouldn't be at odds. Life is too short.'

They slipped into their usual stress-free companionship. She felt elated to have him in her flat and wished she could take photos, but he might get suspicious. Emma told him about her week. She didn't mention that she'd been looking to see if there was new work to be had. She had to escape from this job with Damián first. They lingered over a glass of wine. Neither of them was anxious to end a pleasant evening.

Damián looked at his watch. 'I'd better go, it's almost midnight. Thanks for the meal Emma. I enjoyed it and the cucumbers were perfection!'

'You're welcome! How will you get home? Where is home, by the way? I've a telephone number, but no address.'

He looked sheepish. 'I've a flat in the docklands. Much too big for me on my own, but I bought it years ago. It's worth a lot more today; in fact, it's worth a small fortune. You must visit me one day and get on your hobby horse to criticise my decadent lifestyle, and my white sofas!'

She smiled at him. 'I might have guessed. The devil looks after his own!'

'I need a taxi. Do you have a number?'

Emma ruffled through a drawer and gave him a card. He phoned and was told the taxi would be there in ten minutes. He got up, donned his coat and although his tie hung lopsided, he made no attempt to straighten it.

Emma walked with him to the door. As he opened the door he turned at the last minute and stunned her by leaning down to kiss her briefly; it was a delicious sensation. She gazed at him silently, his soft breath fanning her face, then two startled people were suddenly facing a barrage of flashlights from a crowd of photographers.

Emma gazed at him, and then at them, in shock. She was intensely occupied with the fact that he'd actually kissed her, and she wanted to say something, but couldn't. Damián was more used to the situation. He shoved her gently inside and closed the door, and faced them on his own. Emma stood with her back to the doorway for a few seconds, before she had enough willpower to look through the spy-hole. Damián was standing in the midst of them and an occasional flashlight still lit up the hallway. He gradually edged them towards the top of the stairway. Once there, he made a dash for it, and they followed. Emma mused that he must be very fit to run at the speed he did all the time.

She could tell from the fading noise that he'd drawn them away. She turned and let her body slide down until she was sitting on the floor with her legs stuck out in front of her. She touched her lips with her fingers. Her heart thumped erratically and she told herself it was only his way of showing easy, meaningless affection. It didn't imply anything — that was how he was with all women. She thought briefly about the photographers; how did they know he was here? And what would she find in the newspapers tomorrow morning?

8

Have you seen *The Mirror?*' Emma's mother's voice was almost hysterical. 'I can't believe this is happening to my daughter!'

Emma did. 'Mum, calm down! I haven't seen it yet, but I can guess. Damián had a meal here yesterday, and when he was about to leave, a load of photographers went barmy. It was all perfectly innocent!'

'The headline reads, *The Perfect Secretary — Available Day and Night.*' Emma cringed more than a little at her mother's words. ' . . . and there's a picture of him kissing you!'

'What!' Emma's brain was working overtime. 'Oh . . . That doesn't mean a thing Mum. He was being polite. We're just good friends and friends kiss each other sometimes.'

Her voice was unyielding. 'Damián

Alvarez doesn't kiss anyone without an ulterior motive. He kissed you . . . that's enough for me!'

'Mum this is ridiculous! It was all perfectly innocent. He didn't have an ulterior motive. He's my boss, nothing more. We shared a meal at my flat and when he left the press was waiting.'

'If I was you I'd buy a pair of dark glasses and a coat that reaches the floor, because I don't think you're going to get away with this as easily as you think.'

Emma looked up at the ceiling. 'This is so stupid, Mum. Why don't they just leave him alone? He can't lead a normal life, because they won't let him!'

'Don't worry about him, worry about yourself. You're the one with a reputation to lose. He lost his years ago, if he ever had one!'

Her voice was sharp. 'Oh don't be so old fashioned, Mum!'

'Emma!'

'I'm sorry . . . but it's true. Do you believe me, or do you believe the newspapers? Damián and I have done nothing we should feel embarrassed about. I expect you to support me, not to act like I'm a sultry page-one pin-up who's been entertaining Casanova.'

There was silence at the other end of the line then her mother said, 'You're right! I'm not accusing you of anything; it's just a bit of a shock to see your daughter's face plastered all over *The Daily Mirror* that's all. I haven't heard from your dad yet, I don't suppose the people in work will take long to tell him. Have you heard from him . . . from Damián?'

'No, perhaps he hasn't seen the paper yet. Anyway, he's used to it; Damián probably won't take much notice. Normally I wouldn't be seeing him until tomorrow evening, when we leave for Australia.'

'That may save you. Out of sight, out of mind!'

Emma bit her lip. 'I wonder who told the press. He came back early, so I don't think the paparazzi could have known.' Wrinkling her brows, she had a brainwave. 'I know! It must have been Robert!'

Mrs McKay was still absorbing the effects of the newspaper report; her mind had to lurch to follow the new route. 'Robert? What's Robert got to do with it?'

'That's what I'm going to find out. He came here last night and he met Damián.' Emma heard her parent's doorbell in the background. 'Check if there's a bunch of curious press men before you open the door! I'll phone you later, Mum!'

Emma put the phone down, and it rang immediately again.

'Hello!' Emma recognised the chuckle and his voice. 'It's not funny Damián! You may be used to this sort of thing; I'm not. My mother's up in arms, and anyone who ever knew me now thinks I'm a fast woman, chasing her boss!'

He gave a belly laugh. 'Oh Emma! If you chased me, I wouldn't stand a chance! I'm sorry your mother's upset;

I'll phone her and try to explain.'

Emma blushed, but didn't want to mention his kiss. 'I've already tried, but it doesn't help much. She still thinks I'm beyond help. I think Robert is possibly behind all of this!'

'Robert? You mean Robert of the starched collars?' He sounded really surprised. 'Why do you think that?'

'It's logical! Who else knew you were in my flat? No one expected you back, did they? Robert saw a chance of getting revenge, because he thinks you're to blame that I don't fall on my knees and beg for absolution.' Her anger was mounting and her brain went into top gear. 'Just wait! I'm going to give him a piece of my mind!'

'Whoa! Calm down! Even if he's guilty, what good will your finger-pointing do? He was angry and upset that you'd thrown him out; feel some compassion! He's a frustrated man who tried to lash out — just forget it!'

'No I won't! You're so used bad publicity, you don't care what anyone says anymore; I do! Why should he drag you into it; his anger should be directed exclusively at me. But two can play that game! I'm going to see him!'

Hastily Damián asked, 'Where does he work?'

'In Dowling Street, he's an investment banker in a private bank called Weston & Philby. Don't worry; he's not the sort who'd give me a black eye!' Emma put the phone down before Damián could protest further.

★ ★ ★

Emma had never seen Robert so flustered. He was facing an irate woman who was accusing him of being a press informant at the top of her voice. The noise attracted the attention of other workers in the small establishment. They could hardly fail to hear what was going on. In the doorway, a senior partner was also an interested spectator.

'You're a spiteful, parsimonious,

deplorable, cruel, and petty little man! I've never done anything to hurt you, apart from telling you I didn't want to marry you, and you'd never met Damián Alvarez until last night. How dare you try to drag our names through the mud, just to satisfy your shattered ego!'

Robert pulled at the tie at his neck. It was getting tighter by the minute. 'I don't know what you're talking about!'

Emma leaned forward across the desk and pointed at his chest. 'I'll add 'liar' to the list of your attributes! I'll have you charged with slander.' Emma knew she couldn't prove anything; the press protected their informers.

Robert's flushed face and round eyes spoke for themselves even though he tried to flummox his way out. 'How often do I have to tell you I've had nothing to do with this?'

'I don't believe you Robert. You're despicable! I never want to see you again. Damián was right about one thing though . . . I shouldn't waste my time on you. You're not worth it.' She picked up a mug of coffee, and he watched in horror as she slowly trickled the contents over the tidy piles of papers on his desk.

Emma left; edging past the flabbergasted partner, and girls with amused expressions in the corridor. It would take Robert a long time to climb on to his office pedestal again. It hadn't done much good, but she felt happier. When she came out through the glass entrance door, Damián was leaning nonchalantly against one of the white marble pillars framing the portico.

'Feeling better?'

She grinned. 'Much!

He held out the crook of his arm and she tucked her arm through his.

His smile flashed briefly, dazzling against the olive skin. 'Right! Let's have some breakfast in that bistro; I'm hungry.'

As they hurried across the busy road, he added, 'I've arranged to take your parents out for a meal with us this evening! I explained the best line of defence is attack. If I was having a seedy affair with my assistant, I'd hardly ask her parents out, would I? Your mother thought it was brilliant, and even suggested 'anonymously' informing the press! I persuaded her not to bother! The press will hear about it without any prompting. Who wants to read about me sharing a meal with my assistant's parents? If I was partying at a nightclub with some bunny-girls it would be a different kettle of fish!'

Emma laughed out loud. She now knew without a doubt that she loved him, and on top of everything else, he was a thoroughly nice man.

★   ★   ★

By the time they reached Australia, she'd adjusted to the fact that she loved him. It didn't make it easier to be with him, but at least she didn't have to fight devils all the time. She hid behind Pablo and Carmelita, didn't linger with him alone unless it was unavoidable, and didn't try to grab his attention. She did her job, fitted in with the routine as before, and tried to behave in the same friendly, detached way. She let her fantasy free when she watched him from a distance. She tried to understand why he was the one man on earth with whom she wanted to grow old, but couldn't. She came from another background, they had different characters, but he wakened fierce emotions in her every time she saw him. She didn't know whether to be glad or sorry that he didn't try to repeat the kiss, or that he'd never even mentioned it since.

He won the first tournament. There was a fat cheque at the end of the day, and a picture of Damián in the newspaper smiling like a Cheshire cat. At the press conference she and Carmelita stood at the back and watched how Damián handled the reporters with accustomed skill; he caught Emma's eye and he gave her a knowing grin.

For the next tournament, Emma had hired a house bordering the ocean. Outside the back door was the Pacific. The beach had fine sand and was fringed by tall palms. Life was wonderful; she had work that was well within her capabilities, and she was seeing the world.

The first day went off without a hitch. It wasn't a very prestigious tournament but Damián was enjoying himself. He loved golf — full-stop. The local press printed a huge article about the tournament and about Damián. Pablo told them that a group of female admirers had started to besiege the golf club in the hope of seeing him. Feeling annoyed, but showing nothing, Emma smiled indulgently.

Very early on the second day, Emma threw on a dressing gown and dashed out of the shower when she heard a commotion. She expected to find a reporter. Instead, with mouth half-open, she located a half-naked young woman standing outside Damián's room clutching her clothing. She was yelling at him, and from somewhere inside came a muffled answer.

'But . . . you said you hoped to see me again! I'm sure that's what I heard!'

Damián's voice was getting louder. 'On the golf course, woman! I didn't mean I was inviting you to share my bed!'

The girl stood, clothes over her arm, looking into his room. 'There's no need for you to throw me out. It's humiliating!'

Damián, head tousled and body with a towel wrapped round his hips, appeared at the door. 'How the hell did you get in here? Why are you undressed? And how did you know which room I was in?'

The girl wavered. 'I . . . I followed you home and watched you moving around. The kitchen window was open, and I crept up to wait for you to wake up. I don't need to explain why I'm undressed, do I?'

There was a throaty laugh from

further down the corridor, where Pablo was leaning against the door watching.

Damián pointed to the stairs. 'It's very flattering that you've gone to so much trouble, but I choose my own girlfriends. You know the way out; I suggest you leave . . . right now!'

The girl tossed her blond head. Her lacy red tanga left little to the imagination. The cheeks of her bottom were bobbing about like two firm apples, and her ample breasts were barely confined in a matching bra. The rest of her clothes were still dangling. 'Well . . . phone me if you change your mind. Want my telephone number?'

Damián ran his hand over his face and his glance took in Emma. He grinned wickedly. 'No!'

Emma's pulse increased noticeably at the sight of his muscled body, but she sent him a contemptuous look, and closed her door with unnecessary force. She took time to get dressed; and reminded herself that it was none of her business.

Downstairs, the others were nearly finished breakfast when she joined them. Pablo looked up and winked. Emma fetched a mug of coffee from the machine and put two slices of bread in the toaster. She looked out of the window and studied the palm leaves swaying in the wind. She avoided Damián and started to butter her toast; the least said the better — it may not be his fault, but he attracted trouble in a way that was unbelievable.

Pablo looked at his watch. 'We have to go Damián; we're late!'

Damián took a last gulp of coffee. Slinging a soft blue wool pullover round his shoulders, he got up. 'Emma, about just now . . . '

Emma held up a hand and looked blasé. 'It's none of my business. Even if the town's entire female population parade themselves in front of you in the way God made them, it's absolutely none of my business. I don't under-stand why, but perhaps you ought to think about changing your brand of after-shave?' She took a generous bite of toast and touched the corner of her mouth to re-manoeuvre some of the jam. Clearing her mouth, she continued, 'Would you like me to make some business cards showing how to get to your bedroom; so that women have less trouble to locate you? I hope you manage to keep ahead of your competitors, and the local female population, and that you'll have a successful day! I'll get confirmation of our next scheduled stopover sometime today, and if the girls allow you enough time, you can perhaps take a look at it sometime this evening?'

Pablo's face split in two. He touched his hat and ambled towards the door, a thermos flask in his hand. Damián looked at her through narrowed eyes and departed with him.

They heard the car leaving and Carmelita laughed softly. 'Oh Emma! It wasn't his fault. You shouldn't taunt him. He was wild but he's calmed down a lot.'

Emma's eyes sparkled. 'Has he? His casual attitude automatically attracts trouble. Why did that girl think he wanted to see her again? I expect he threw her a couple of smiles, and that was enough. She'd read the articles saying he's open to romantic adventure, and decided to look him up. If women believe he's casual about sex, then it leads to this kind of thing. It's his own fault!'

Carmelita's shoulders shook, and the bangles jingled. 'Oh, I don't think he's ever been casual about sex. I won't say he's lived like a monk, but the idea that he pops in and out of strange beds like a ferret is wide of the mark.'

Emma shrugged her shoulders. 'It's none of my business.'

★　★　★

The sky was blue in a cloudless sky. Emma sent off some enquiries, printed out various schedules, and wallowed in the luxury of a swim in the ocean. After changing, Emma went to help Carmelita. Emma reckoned it wouldn't be long before the men came home. She was slicing red peppers when the telephone rang. They didn't get many calls, because few people knew where they were.

'Hello!'

'Emma!' Damián sounded strange.

'Damián? Going to be late?'

His voice cracked and he sounded like he was gasping for air. 'No . . . no. There's been an accident. Pablo is on his way to hospital; meet me at the St. John's Hospital on Lawrence Street with Carmelita, as soon as possible!'

The surprise nearly floored her. Emma pulled herself together and tried to remain calm. 'An accident? What happened?'

'A car crash; a drunk drove into the side of our car. Pablo is unconscious, and they think he may have internal injuries.'

The thought that they could have been killed crossed her mind. She pulled herself together. 'We'll be there as soon as possible. Are . . . are you all right?'

'Some cuts and bruises; I'd change places if I could.'

'Steady! One step at a time! Wait to see what the doctors say.'

Carmelita was listening. She came towards Emma. 'Is it Pablo?'

Emma nodded. 'There's been a car crash, and Pablo's been taken to hospital.' Tears gathered in Carmelita's eyes. Emma reached out and embraced her. 'The injuries might not be too bad; he's unconscious, but that's usually a temporary thing.'

Emma put her aside gently and reached for the telephone book She began to flick through the pages looking for a taxi. 'Anything in the oven?' Carmelita shook her head silently. She was as white as a ghost and looked lost. 'Get your things, and take a cardigan. We'll go straight to the hospital.'

When they arrived, Emma took a couple of minutes to find out where

Pablo had been taken, and they finally found the long corridor where Damián was sitting. He looked a bundle of misery. His legs apart, he was resting his arms on his upper thighs and his head was cradled in his hands. When he saw them, he got up jerkily and held out his arms to Carmelita. Once Carmelita was lost in the depth of his shoulder, he looked at Emma. His eyes were full of worry. There were some dark bruises, and minor cuts on his cheek and forehead.

He said 'They're checking for internal bleeding. From what I understand, that's one of the biggest hazards; it would mean emergency surgery'. He held Carmelita from him. 'He was unconscious when I last saw him. The doctor promised to inform me as soon as they knew anything definite.'

Carmelita answered him in Spanish and tears ran down her face.

He looked fierce and gripped her shoulders tightly when he answered. 'No . . . he's not going to die! It was a

158

bad crash but no one has said anything like that.'

Damián guided Carmelita back to the row of chairs. Emma noticed that he was limping slightly. She went to get coffees with extra sugar.

Emma sent up a silent prayer that everything would be all right. She walked to the end of the corridor and looked out of the window. It seemed a lifetime until she heard the swing-doors. Damián and Carmelita were already on their feet; Emma joined them. Wearing a white coat and holding some medical charts, the doctor sounded reassuring.

'The good news is that there doesn't seem to be any internal bleeding. The ultra scans are clear, and his pulse rate is now fairly normal, as is his breathing. He's broken a wrist-bone, a leg in two places, and a couple of ribs — that was what made me wonder if the spleen was damaged. The air-bag seems to have absorbed the impact. There's quite a bit of bruising but . . .

things considered he's lucky. He's still unconscious, and I'll be happier when he comes round. A colleague of mine is dealing with the broken bones at the moment and then we'll put him into intensive care until he regains consciousness. He still needs careful surveillance for a few days but on the whole I'm optimistic.' He gave Carmelita a gentle smile. 'Once he's in intensive care, you can see him. I know that relatives like to stay with patients and I have no objection. It's difficult to guess when he'll regain consciousness — it could be an hour, it could be a day, so I'd advise you not to tire yourself out in the process.'

Carmelita's eyes were sparkling with tears of relief. She grasped the doctor's hand. 'Thank you. Thank you!'

The doctor nodded. Gripping the papers in his hand more firmly he turned to go. He gave Damián a closer scrutiny. 'You're the golfer, aren't you? Your photo was plastered across the sports section yesterday.'

Damián nodded; his lips were a tight line. 'And that's my caddy in there!'

Understandingly the doctor looked more closely. 'You seem to have some cuts and bruising yourself. Were you in the same car? Has anyone taken a look at you?'

Damián shook his head, still agitated. 'It's not so important. Don't worry about me.'

'Get yourself checked out — if you don't, you might end up with bigger problems later. Delaying treatment is never as effective as doing something immediately. Your friend isn't out of the wood yet, but he's on the way!' The stethoscope jogged against his chest, he did an about-turn, and vanished through the swing doors.

They all felt slightly better, knowing that the news was bad, but not horrific.

Emma asked. 'Exactly what happened?'

Damián looked at her and his lips thinned again perceptibly. 'We were just driving into the middle of the crossroad

161

when some drunk drove through the red lights and rammed into us from the side. He'll have to answer for it, but it won't help Pablo much.'

They were silent as they sat down to wait for news again. Thirty minutes later a friendly nurse came for Carmelita. 'If you come with me, I'll take you to see your husband now.'

Carmelita jumped up.

Emma gave her a quick hug. 'One, or both of us, will be back later. Do you need anything?'

Carmelita shook her head. 'Now that I know he'll be all right nothing else seems important.'

Emma smiled. 'Of course, but if he takes a long time to come round, you'll need a rest. We'll come to take you home whenever you call!' She gave Carmelita her mobile phone and a piece of paper. 'Here's the telephone number; just punch that in and press the green button.'

Damián joined them, put his hand on her shoulder and gave her a reassuring smile. 'He'll pull through Carmelita! Pablo is tough.'

Carmelita's lips were shaking, but she smiled before she followed the uniformed nurse. Her mind was on Pablo.

When she'd gone from sight, Emma turned her attention to Damián.

'You're limping That doctor was right; you ought to get it checked. We'll go back to the outpatient department. Can you walk without pain? I'll find you a wheelchair if you like. In fact, it might be better for you.'

He lifted his eyebrows and shook his head determinedly. 'It's not that bad. I'm just so glad that Pablo is not on the danger list.'

Resolutely Emma said, 'Let's find a doctor. Even if you got off more lightly than Pablo, you were in the crash too.'

A relatively short time later, Emma got up from where she'd been waiting for him in a busy reception area. Damián emerged from one of the treatment rooms with some plasters on his face and he was still walking with a limp, but he looked more comfortable.

'No real damage. My kneecap is badly bruised, cuts and bruises and a bit of a cracked rib!'

Emma was concerned. 'Your knee? Did they X-ray it?'

With dry amusement in his voice, he said, 'They X-rayed everything! They told me to keep my weight off my knee for a couple of days, and to get some treatment. Let's get a taxi, go to the hire-car company and get a replacement car. Carmelita should get in touch soon and ask us to pick her up. It's a good thing you can drive, Emma!'

9

Pablo regained consciousness during the night. They kept him in intensive care until the following afternoon, and then he spent a week under observation so Emma was very busy. She cancelled all immediate schedules, and drove Damián and Carmelita back and forth to the hospital. When Carmelita wasn't with Pablo, Damián was, so Emma kept her visits short. She thought that Pablo might be grateful for some peace and quiet!

The day before Pablo came home, Damián and Emma drove Carmelita to the hospital and left her at the entrance. They took time to find somewhere close at hand to park. Damián was still limping, and Emma had learned to adjust her pace to his. When they reached Pablo's room, Pablo had his arm around Carmelita, and had tears in his eyes. Emma's heart plunged, but then she saw Carmelita's expression was not one of sadness, but one of joy and calmed down again instantly.

Damián looked at Pablo. 'What's wrong?'

Pablo grinned like a Cheshire cat and wiped his cheeks with the back of his hand. 'Nothing! I'm going to be a father!'

'What!' Damián clapped Pablo on the back. Pablo winced and grinned. 'Oh, sorry! But congratulations!'

Emma embraced Carmelita and, giving her a kiss on the cheek, she said, 'Brilliant! I'm so happy for you both. How long have you known?'

Eyes still twinkling, Carmelita said, 'Four weeks, but I wanted to be sure before I told Pablo. I'll be forty this year. I went to a specialist when we were in Spain and I phoned for the results today. So far, everything is fine! I can't believe it — I'd given up hope!'

Emma crossed to Pablo and kissed him on his cheek. She didn't need to say anything, Damián had Carmelita in his arms and the room vibrated with torrents of happy Spanish.

★ ★ ★

When Pablo eventually came home, Carmelita wouldn't let him do anything, and Pablo kept insisting she should sit down and rest. Emma extended the rental for the bungalow and the next two weeks was a bit like an unexpected holiday. Damián's knee improved a little although progress was slow, so she cancelled his schedule for at least a month. He decided to go back to Europe for specialist treatment. A lot of Damián and Pablo's talk circled around who was going to caddy for Damián in the future because Pablo said he wanted to be around when his child grew up. Damián understood.

The two men spent a lot of time discussing, telephoning around and checking. Finally they decided a young caddy named Kent Ward would be right. Kent's present boss was leaving the circuit at the end of the year, and he was looking for a new job. Pablo made the first tentative contacts, and they arranged a meeting. Damián already knew him by sight, and Kent agreed to accompany Damián for a trial period of three months when Damián rejoined the circuit. Emma wondered how Pablo felt after being at Damián's side for so many years.

One day Damián returned from a phone conversation with his brother. 'Julio asked why we don't come home as soon as possible. It's not a bad idea, is it? I expect you'd love to go home Carmelita?'

Carmelita's brow furrowed. 'Yes, I would, but only if the doctors say Pablo is fit for such a long journey.'

Damián lifted his hand. 'That goes without saying.'

Pablo said, 'I'd rather be on my own patio than here on the other side of the world; I'm ready to go.'

Damián nodded. 'We'll discuss things

with the doctor tomorrow.'

Carmelita hitched her hands to her hips and her silver earrings jangled. 'And I'll be there, to make sure you ask all the right questions!'

A smile cut Damián's face in two. 'Oh, some other very interesting news. Julio said that Elena Mendez has filed for divorce from her husband on the grounds of their incompatibility.'

Emma's fingers were digging in the sand, and her grip tightened. She looked up and met Pablo's eyes; Emma suddenly realised he knew that she was in love with Damián. She hoped no one else did.

Her heart sank and she had a sense of misery and loss. Elena was planning to pick up where she and Damián had left off all those years ago! Perhaps they'd settled their future during the stay at the hotel? A suffocating blanket of gloom covered her. She got up from her knees and brushed the sand from her shorts. Looking at no one in particular, she said. 'I'm going to wash my hair and do the shopping. Anyone want something?'

She was almost out of hearing by the time Carmelita shouted, 'Toilet paper!'

Emma sat in the car looking over a stretch of sand bordering the sea; she didn't register where she was. It could've been in a busy shopping precinct or a desert island — it didn't make any difference. Even though she'd already known she couldn't go on living with him indefinitely without giving herself away, it hurt enormously to know she'd have to leave. If he'd never stopped loving Elena, the way was now free for them. She wasn't the kind of woman he deserved, but if she was his choice . . .

She closed her eyes, her heart ached with pain. She gulped hard, and hot tears flowed freely down her cheeks. She sat in lonely silence and felt utterly miserable. Their tightly-knit little group was breaking up anyway — her departure would give Damián a chance to make a completely fresh start. This was a perfect moment to back out. Emma's head bowed, and her body slumped, as sobs rocked her body and she thought about her future without him.

★ ★ ★

The knowledge that she was sharing the last days hung over her like a soap bubble about to burst. The doctor gave them the go-ahead. Two days before their departure, Damián asked. 'Coming to Spain? You can go home later to see your family.'

He speared some salad with his fork and watched her as he chewed.

A suffocating sensation tightened her throat. She gave him a choked laugh. 'No. This time, I go home straight away. The first stop is Heathrow, and there's no pressing reason to go to Spain, is there?'

He hesitated and Emma was mesmerised by his dark eyes. Finally, he shrugged. 'But you'll join us later?'

Emma didn't answer and reached forward to cut a piece of camembert and take a piece of bread.

Carmelita began to talk; she was delighted to be going home. Emma was pleased for her and Pablo; their coming baby was now the centre of their universe. To Emma's relief Damián didn't press for an answer.

As expected, the flight was long and tiring, especially for Pablo. When they reached Heathrow, there was a wheel-chair waiting for him. Damián was still walking with a limp. Damián and Emma walked behind the other two, until 'In Transit' passengers parted from those staying in London.

Moving aside not to obstruct other passengers Emma put down her cabin bag and briefcase. She hugged Pablo and kissed his leathered cheek. 'Good luck! I hope your plaster comes off soon!'

He smiled up at her. 'So do I! Take care!'

'I will.' She turned to Carmelita and

gave her a hug and a kiss. 'You take care of yourself and your baby. I'll be in touch.'

Carmelita nodded and returned her hug.

Emma hurried them along. 'You have an hour before the flight leaves for Spain; you'd better find the right boarding gate as soon as possible.'

Carmelita turned back to the wheelchair, they moved off down a long corridor. Emma watched them. It left her and Damián alone; she turned to him.

She spoke with quiet but desperate firmness; she'd been rehearsing what to say. Drawing a deep breath, she met his gaze straight on. 'Damián, I've decided this is as good a moment as any to tell you that I'd like to resign.'

His smile disappeared and he stiffened as though she'd struck him. 'You're doing what? Leaving us, just like that?'

She bit her lip and after a second, she said calmly, 'Yes. The car accident and

Carmelita's pregnancy has changed everything.' She lifted her chin. 'You're reorganising your life — getting a new caddy. I'm fond of Pablo and Carmelita, they're lovely, but I don't think I want to be part of a new set-up. The job was only temporary anyway, wasn't it?'

He replied with heavy irony and his jaw thrust forward. 'Was it? I can't remember saying it was a temporary job.' He paused. 'You realise you're leaving me in the lurch, and that you're making a difficult situation more impossible?'

Emma was humiliatingly conscious of his scrutiny and remained silent.

'Perhaps I should have said nothing would change, but I presumed you realised that.' He clenched his mouth tighter and glowered at the occasional passenger who gave them a curious glance as they passed. His eyes were stormy. 'Do we have to talk about this here and now! In an airport corridor?' He thrust his hands in his pocket and hunched his shoulders.

She froze for a moment, her breath caught in her lungs. An unwelcome blush crept to her cheeks and she answered in a rush of words. 'It wouldn't make any difference if we talked about it sitting in comfortable armchairs in the lounge at the Ritz. My mind is made up. If it helps, I'll organise your schedules for you . . . from a distance, until you have a replacement. I'm sure that you'll find someone else soon, or you could even do it yourself, just as you did before I came.'

There was more than a suggestion of annoyance in his eyes and his tongue was heavy with sarcasm. 'How very kind of you! You drop me like a hot potato, and then pretend you're concerned about how I'll manage!'

She snapped her mouth shut, and the words wedged in her throat. She took a sharp breath; the blood was siphoned from her face. 'Don't Damián! Don't blame me because circumstances have changed. Let's remain friends, please! I don't want to put you on the spot, but I don't want to continue either.'

He gave her a look of utter disbelief. 'Friends? Huh! Is that really what you want, for us to be friends? That's not possible.' A chill hung in the air.

She tried to retain some flecks of affability although she saw a distinct hardening of his eyes. She pressed her lips together and managed to reply in an even tone. 'Do you want me to handle everything until you've found a solution, or not? If you don't, you should take the notebook, credit cards and everything else now.' She held out the briefcase.

He leaned towards her, his eyes cold. 'Do what you like with it! I couldn't care less.'

He glared at her for a moment, before he turned to follow others going down the corridor. After a few steps, he suddenly wheeled and came back. Crushing her to him, he pressed his mouth to hers. The kiss was challenging and rewarding. Her senses reeled as if she'd been short-circuited, and his nearness kindled feelings of fire. An expression of satisfaction showed in his eyes. 'Not completely without emotion are you? I always thought there was more than professional propriety in you somewhere.'

He let go, and turned away, to stride down the empty corridor without a backward glance. He disappeared and Emma righted herself. She let her fingers drift over her lips. Her breath quickened and her cheeks burned. She set her chin in a stubborn line, although she began to feel a sort of wretchedness she'd never known before. Reluctantly, she moved towards Passport Control. Emma wanted to cry, but was determined not to. She hadn't expected it to be easy. When she'd reclaimed her suitcase, she went to the nearest ladies. She splashed cold water on her ashen face, and dried it with a paper towel. She recalled a poem they'd learned in school.

I hold it true, whate'er befall;

I feel it, when I sorrow most;
'Tis better to have loved and lost,
Than never to have loved at all.

★   ★   ★

The first days were hard going. She had to ease the pain and accept the loss. Some people could display their misery with ease, Emma chose to hide it from a world that couldn't understand.

Even a visit to her parents was a mountain to climb because her mother brought Damián's name into the conversation several times. Meeting him face to face had removed a lot of misgivings and even her father seemed reassured. Emma told them about the car accident, and Carmelita's baby, but she didn't tell them that she'd quit the job.

She didn't hear from Damián and presumed he'd rejoin the circuit as soon as his knee was healed. She knew he wasn't fit enough yet, she read so in the sport section. She tried to ignore the briefcase and started to search for work — a job that would leave her no time for personal misery. She found one — to catalogue a library in a deserted mansion in Dorset. It'd take several weeks. There was a resident house-keeper and a gardener. It was just what she needed. She phoned her mother and told her she'd left Damián and had a new job.

Her mother was silent for a few seconds. 'Oh . . . I know I was doubtful about him, but now I've met him he's not at all what I expected. You liked him too, didn't you?'

Emma brushed the tears away with her hand. 'Yes. I decided it was the right moment to leave so that he can build up a completely new team.' She put her hand over the phone, and shut her eyes to concentrate for a second. Her mother didn't have much chance to comment because Emma managed to divert attention by telling her about her new job.

10

That evening Carmelita phoned Emma for a chat. After the usual greetings and Emma's enquiry about how Carmelita was feeling, Carmelita said, 'Come for a visit! There are lots of special offers; it won't cost you much and we'll pick you up. Pablo's plaster is coming off on Thursday. His bones have healed fast. He's looking forward to it like a child at Christmas. So am I; being immobile makes him so grumpy.'

Emma heard Carmelita's earrings jingling. 'That's understandable! He's always been active. A leg in plaster must be hell for him.' Emma noticed that Carmelita hadn't mentioned Damián. 'You know that I've left Damián? I thought he ought to build up a whole new team.'

Carmelita was silent for a second. 'I haven't seen him, but Pablo has. We were a good team and got on well, didn't we? He'll probably find it tough for a while to adjust to new people, but he seems to get on okay with Kent. Pablo didn't ask why you left. You know Pablo; he's never pushed him for information.'

'Yes, that's why they got on.'

Emma told her about the new job she was starting soon.

'Then come this weekend? Once you start, you'll not have time for a while.'

Emma laughed. 'I'd always find time for you. I'd love to see you, and you know it!' Carmelita and Pablo had a vineyard in a completely different area of Spain to the hotel, so Emma reasoned that there was little chance of bumping into Damián. 'I'll find out if there's a flight and phone you back.'

It only took her a few minutes. She gave Carmelita the details and looked forward to seeing them. It was a bright spot on a gloomy horizon. When this new job finished, she'd find another. Keeping occupied was vital; one day she would return to normality and she wouldn't spend all her time thinking about Damián.

★   ★   ★

Getting off the plane reminded her of last time. Walking towards them, she smiled easily for the first time for ages. Pablo was walking again and he caught her hand in a warm clasp.

'Hi Emma!'

She laughed. 'Hi Pablo! I'm glad to see you without a plaster. What about the other injuries? Everything okay?'

He nodded, and Emma relaxed.

Carmelita enfolded her in her soft bosom and laughed softly. 'It's nice to have you here. We've missed you!'

They drove northward, and were soon in the middle of wine-growing country. When Pablo left the main highway, they drove down a bumpy track and halted in front of a box-shaped building. There was a wonderful view of the countryside and vines dominated the landscape. Emma took a deep breath of the clear air and held her head up to the sun's weakening rays. 'Oh, this is wonderful! How could you ever leave here in the first place?'

Pablo rubbed his hand across his mouth and scanned the hills. 'At first it was because of money, then because of friendship, and finally because of habit.' He laughed. 'I'm glad I'm here and this is where I want our child to grow up.'

Emma nodded; the wind grabbed her rust coloured hair, and pulled it out of shape. She tried vainly to lodge it behind her ears. 'It's really lovely here. Is it always so windy?'

Carmelita came to stand next to her, her comfortable clothes flapping in the wind. 'Sometimes, but not often. Pablo's brother is our next neighbour; he lives over there.' She pointed to a house a distance away. 'Come in, and I'll make you a good cup of English tea.' She dropped her arm along Emma's shoulder and pulled her along.

'You need feeding up; you've shadows under your eyes and lost weight!'

She laughed. 'I've missed your cooking!' Emma was glad to be with two people that she had grown to love in a special way.

It was a lovely weekend; it was almost like old times — only Damián was missing. They went for walks, visited the nearby market town and lazed on the terrace. She drank Pablo's wine and was impressed. They visited Pablo's brother one afternoon and Emma met his family. On her final evening when Carmelita was busy in the kitchen, she gave Pablo the briefcase.

'You'll be seeing Damián sometime?'

He nodded. 'We're keeping in touch.'

'Next time you see him, will you give him this? I tried to hand it over at the airport, but he was too angry. The computer contains all sorts of important information. If it fell into the wrong hands, someone could manipulate his finances. Tell him to delete everything if he's not going to use it again. If he doesn't know how, Julio will do it for him.' She rested her elbows on the table and managed to sound quite casual. 'How is he?'

Pablo leaned back.

'Health-wise he's able to play a full round of golf comfortably without any problems. He hasn't made a move to get back on the circuit yet. I don't know why. The longer he takes out, the quicker his name will drop down the ratings.'

She looked at the rough grain of the solid dining table and drew imaginary lines with her fingers. 'Perhaps Elena is more of an attraction for him than golf at the moment?'

Pablo shifted uneasily in his chair and made a surly grunt. 'Elena? I didn't see her around anywhere, but I suppose it's possible. She threw him aside for money and I don't think Damián will forget that — but more than that, don't think he's really in love with her either.'

There was a lump in her throat, but she managed. 'I do. If he loves her, he'll forgive and forget.'

He studied her silently for a moment, and decided to say what had been stuck in his throat for a while. 'Only someone who loves him could say that.' Emma looked away. Pablo reached forward and covered her hand with his, and said. 'Life isn't fair sometimes? I don't think he appreciates what he's losing.'

Without actually admitting anything but knowing that Pablo knew, she said. 'You can't miss what you don't know exists. It's just as well; it would embarrass him. You . . . you won't ever mention anything, will you Pablo? Please don't, not even a hint, ever!'

He shrugged. 'I've only given advice when he asked for it.'

She straightened her back and gave him a shaky smile. 'Good! I hope he finds happiness. He's a nice person.'

He didn't want to upset her and changed the subject, 'Tell me about this new job, then . . . '

★ ★ ★

186

She'd arrived a couple of days ago. The housekeeper was a friendly, helpful widow and the only other employee was an elderly gardener.

It was a wonderful autumn day, full of reds, yellows and gold. The house was an elegant Georgian mansion, but the upkeep had finally forced the family to put it up for sale. As she looked out of the eight-paned window, she almost regretted that she'd too much to do. The wind was throwing the leaves around in small whirlwinds of colour. Her breath clouded the pane, the gardens must have been very impressive in the past; they were still beautiful in a neglected way. She drew a heart on the misted glass and turned towards the desk. She picked up a bundle of books she'd just finished listing and packed them away. Looking at her watch, she reckoned she had enough time to finish one more lot, before she went to the kitchen for a mid-morning coffee break.

In the beautiful ornate cream and gold library, Emma gathered another batch of leather-bound books from one of the half-empty shelves. They were covered in a thin layer of dust. She carried them across to the desk near the windows where she dusted them carefully with a soft cloth before listing them. She looked up when Mrs Moss, came in.

'Emma! There's someone to see you.'

Emma left the volumes strewn haphazardly across the desk. 'For me? Who could that be?' There weren't too many names to chose from. Hardly anyone knew she was here.

'I didn't catch the name; it was foreign. A very good-looking young man, tanned . . . tall with very dark hair . . . well-dressed.'

Emma's heartbeat began to race, and wave after wave of shock slapped at her. The description left her without a doubt. She brushed some dust from her skirt, and straightened the turtle-necked pullover. 'Where is he?'

'I asked him to come in, but he said he'd rather wait outside. He's behind the house, near the orangery.'

Emma rushed down the corridor leading to the entrance hall. She opened a door on the left and entered the largest sitting room on the ground floor. Crossing it quickly, and not paying attention to the fine proportions or the select furniture, she wrenched open the French windows. She reached the gravel pathway circumnavigating the house and her footsteps crunched on the surface.

Her heart did a somersault when she saw Damián. His hands were stuck in his coat pockets; the ends of a red scarf flew about unhindered in the wind. He was striding impatiently up and down.

Although the wind was chilly, Emma didn't notice it. Feeling breathless and finding it impossible to steady her erratic pulse, her mind was a mixture of delight, shock, and of unspoken hope. Why had he come? She came to a stop, her heart jumping madly about in her chest, as she stared at him.

He closed the distance between

them, studying her intensely. His expression did nothing to quieten her emotions. His voice was honeyed. 'Hello, Emma!'

His voice sent a ripple of need through her. She blurted out breathlessly. 'What on earth are you doing here? How did you find me?' Her brain was slowly beginning to function again. 'There's nothing wrong with Carmelita or the baby? Or Pablo?'

There was a trace of laughter in his voice. 'No, nothing's wrong with Carmelita or Pablo. I saw them both yesterday.' He paused. 'Pablo told me about you and this job. He didn't have the address, so I phoned your mother. I drove down this morning and had a hell of a job to find you — the house is hidden away like a state secret!'

As she gradually adjusted to having him close again, the words began to flow more easily. 'Yes, I know. I took a taxi from the station and, luckily, the taxi driver knew the way. If I'd driven down, I wouldn't have found it straight off either.' Her voice was calm and her gaze steady. 'I visited Pablo and Carmelita recently and gave him your briefcase. Did you get it?'

He nodded and said in a tone of velvet edged with steel. 'You visited them; and couldn't even phone me?' His dark eyes never left hers for an instant.

She was unwilling to face him, and unable to turn away. She tried to control her swirling emotions. 'After the way we parted at the airport, I didn't think it was a good idea. I assumed you wouldn't want to see me. Pablo said he saw you, so it was a perfect way for me to return the briefcase.'

With a flicker in his brilliant eyes, he replied tersely. 'You could have phoned me and asked me to collect it personally. It's not that far from the hotel to Pablo's.' He ran his hand through his hair, and the tone of his voice mellowed. 'Look, I admit I over-reacted at the airport, but your decision floored me; I never reckoned with you leaving. You know me, I blow my top one minute, and often regret it the next.' Pausing he gazed at her speculatively. 'I think it's odd that if you were in Spain that you didn't want to give me it personally. It's not usually how you function!'

The wind was playing havoc with her hair, and Damián was playing havoc with her heart. 'You surely didn't come all this way to find out why?' She felt how pink flooded her cheeks and hoped he'd attribute it to the playful wind. She shrugged to hide her confusion and crossed her arms defiantly. She tried to look relaxed but her spirit was in chaos. With quiet emphasis, she said. 'The laptop contains very important data; I didn't want it to fall into the wrong hands. I was glad to hand it over to someone we both trust . . . ' She swallowed hard, and added, 'I didn't want to drag you away from anything important.'

He looked puzzled and asked matter-of-factly. 'You didn't want to drag me away? From what? The hotel? Golf? Julio? My parents?' Tilting his head to the side, he added, 'By the way, things are fine now; thanks to you . . . as my mother informed me!'

Emma took a moment to steady her thoughts, and then met his eyes again. 'Don't credit me with too much. Your mother was unhappy. I just encouraged her.' Under his steady scrutiny, she couldn't think straight and her emotions were all haywire.

His jaw was thrust forward and his tone was smooth and mechanical. 'My mother insists your encouragement tipped the scales.'

Emma made an indefinable gesture. 'She cared too much not to try. The main thing is you're back on good terms.' Trying to control the conversation, she asked. 'How's your knee? The newspapers are wondering why you're not back on the circuit yet.'

He commented irritably. 'Let them wonder! My golf is okay, and Kent and I get along fine. I'll go back when I'm ready, and not before. Stop changing the subject! I'm still waiting to hear why you didn't phone. I can't believe this has anything to do with the airport episode. I may be quick tempered, but you've always coped. I'm willing to swear there's some other reason you're avoiding me; you like things organised and rounded-off.'

The blood pounded in her temples; she decided to throw caution to the wind. What difference did it make? She'd probably never see him again. Her lips were dry and she cleared her throat. When she answered, her voice sounded stiff. 'I didn't want to butt in, because of Elena.'

He looked puzzled, and asked. 'Elena? You're talking about Elena Mendez?'

She nodded and focussed her attention on a blurred point on the orangery roof, above his head. She struggled with the uncertainty of not having the right words ready. 'I . . . I presumed . . . presumed that now she's getting a

194

divorce that you'd be pairing up again. I guessed she'd get annoyed if you left, just to pick up a notebook from an ex-assistant.' The colour in her face heightened.

He regarded her quizzically for a moment and then his voice was hoarse with frustration. 'Do you mean to say you decided to avoid me because of Elena?'

She clenched her mouth tight and then answered in a rush of words. 'To be honest, she was the reason I left. I didn't want to be part of a setup consisting of Kent, you, Elena and me! I've a feeling she doesn't like me and . . . ' Emma looked at him defiantly. 'To be honest the sentiment is mutual. It wouldn't work, so I got out before I was forced out.' As casually as she could manage she continued, 'I'm sure Elena wouldn't have understood if I'd dragged you away to collect a briefcase connected with work.'

Baffled, he just stared and then he asked in a contemptuous tone. 'May I ask why you think, that I think, Elena is so almighty important?'

A tumble of confused thoughts assailed her. She fidgeted with the folds of her skirt. 'I . . . I just do! I know you were a pair when you were younger, and she was obviously still attracted. You seemed to spend a lot of time together. She came to the flamenco evening and you played golf together all the time. You were delighted when Julio said she was getting divorced, I presumed . . . ' Her stomach knotted and she waited.

His voice had a staccato edge. 'You presumed that I'm still carrying a torch for Elena?' Emma was taken by surprise when his face suddenly crumpled and he threw back his head to let out a peal of laughter. 'Emma, you're jealous; otherwise you wouldn't be so blind!'

Emma bristled. She didn't want to give herself away, and looked around the garden. 'I'm not blind and I'm certainly not jealous! Don't be ridiculous!'

The beginning of a smile tipped the corners of his mouth. 'Have you ever seen me flirting with Elena? Have you seen me running after her? I don't love her. I don't think I ever did! I didn't invite her to the flamenco outing, she more or less invited herself. I arranged that just for you, but you spent the time sleeping and blowing your nose instead! Keeping her at arm's length seemed to make her more determined.'

He ran his fingers through the thick black mass of hair. 'I might have looked pleased when Julio told me about her applying for divorce but that wasn't happiness — it was amusement. I figured she was throwing away the security she had, hoping to catch a bigger fish when she's free again.'

He dug his hands deeper in his pockets and sounded serious. 'Emma, I shut her out of my life more than fifteen years ago. I'm polite when we meet, but she means nothing to me. Why do you pick up all the wrong signals and ignore the proper ones?' His hands came out of his pockets, where they'd been hiding, and he reached out for her. There was still amusement in his eyes. Touching her trembling lips with a finger and seeing the doubt in her tawny eyes, he pulled her roughly into the circle of his arms. 'I have been immeasurably and constantly miserable since we parted. I've spent days wondering how to get you back into my life. I can't live without you!'

Her brain registered that he was watching closely. There were lines of concentration along his brow; he was nervous! Emma stood frozen, searching for the right words. His nearness kindled feelings of fire and she studied his lips longingly. He fulfilled her longings and finally kissed her. The feeling sent the pit of her stomach into a wild swirl and was more seductive than she cared to admit. Emma quivered and felt her knees weaken as his lips recaptured hers, and became more demanding. Her own response was eager and desire surged through her veins. She managed to surface long enough to gather her thoughts.

He looked down at her almost triumphant and leaned forward to hold her tighter. 'You do love me! Admit it!'

Her cheeks burned. 'Damián! Stop it! I am not an infatuated admirer, begging for your attention. Stop play-acting with me! I'm not going to turn out as one of your short-lived bed mates. I told you that before. I believe love should be for a lifetime, you think love is a giddy adventure.' He didn't loosen his grip and Emma found it was hard to remain coherent when he was so close.

His expression stunned her for a moment when he replied. 'I'm not playing at love! I've never been so serious about anything, in the whole of my life.' He managed to look sheepish as he admitted. 'I've been wild in the past, but I swear I've never felt like this about anyone before. I love you! I'd given up looking for love until after I walked into your library and met you. I must have fallen in love when you hid me in that office without really thinking about the consequences. Have you ever wondered why I employed you in the first place? I could have employed a professionally trained public relation manager if I thought I needed one, or at least somebody who understood something about the world of golf.'

Emma's eyes widened. It was true; she knew he could've employed someone professional to do what she did.

His eyes were lively and sparkled. 'One thing I've found out is there's no point in pretending you're in love if you're not. The girls I met always knew where they stood; I was never a liar. I followed a gut feeling when I persuaded Pablo and Carmelita to give your idea a trial. I soon figured out why I wanted you around — I wanted you as a permanent part of my life.' The breath caught in Emma's throat. 'I knew I'd have the devil's own job to convince you I was serious. I really messed things up in the States that time. Folly and frustration got my pictures plastered all over the newspaper next day and pushed you further away than ever. I decided the only way was to give you time to know me better. I hoped that you'd grow to love me.

'Those last days in Spain on our own, gave me some hope. Then the car accident happened and everything went haywire. It was hard to accept Pablo was leaving but I understood his motives — but when you dumped me at the airport it was a kick in the stomach. Instead of admitting how I felt, and leaving it to fate, I got mad and stormed off, only to regret it the moment I was half way down the corridor. I came back, but you'd already disappeared. Since then, I've never been so miserable in the whole of my life. I love you, and I want to spend the rest of my life proving it — if you'll let me!'

Her breathing was irregular, and she was trying to hold on to reality. 'Why am I different than any of the others you've met?'

He shook his head impatiently. 'Forget the press stories! I'm explaining that tomorrow, next month, next year, and forever, is unthinkable, empty, and pointless unless you're at my side, sharing my life.' He gazed at her with eyes full of fire. 'Trust me! I've a feeling we belong together — you're the missing half of me that's always been missing.'

'But . . . ' She spluttered. 'You've never hinted you were attracted to me in any way! Or that I was special!'

He tilted his head to the side; tongue in cheek he said, 'That's how you wanted things; what you expected wasn't it? If I'd acted besotted, I wouldn't have seen you for the dust! I thought I'd blown it that evening I came to your flat, lost control, and kissed you, but luckily the press distracted you and that glossed things over. I didn't want to rush my fences. You were always busy fighting my past ghosts. I knew you'd think I was only interested in a romp between the sheets or a short-lived love affair. I was certain it'd take time to convince you how serious I was — I was willing to wait.'

He looked so sincere that Emma didn't have a single qualm. There was a maddening hint of arrogance about him, but he had the key to unlock her heart and he alone could fill it with contentment and happiness. Slowly bubbling inside was a feeling that made her want to whoop. She'd always felt right in his company; they'd always felt right together. She was extremely conscious of his virile appeal and no other man had ever had the same effect on her before.

'I want to spend my life with you Emma. I want us to have a family. I want you there at the beginning of my day and at the end. I need you otherwise my life will have no meaning.'

She stared wordlessly. Intense astonishment and satisfaction touched her pale face as she looked into the dark eyes. She liked what she saw, and slowly her expression mirrored his. She felt complete contentment and real happiness flow through her.

With laughing eyes, he added. 'I know I can never measure up to Robert, but if you give me the chance I might turn out to be a passable husband!' Reclaiming her lips, he crushed her to him, and with no hesitation, she kissed him back with a hunger that belied her outward appearance. She was almost shocked at her own eager response to his lips, but she didn't need to pretend anymore and she buried her face in his neck. He kissed the tip of her nose, and kissed her eager mouth again, his hands pressing her to his body. He opened his coat and wrapped them together. 'You're getting cold! Come here!'

She settled herself against his warmth and her emotions whirled and skidded. She couldn't drag her attention from the expression in his eyes.

His smile was boyishly affectionate and full of love. 'That's better! You're where you belong!'

Emma sighed. 'I love you Damián. I have for weeks but I didn't want to get hurt. I'll never be happy with a meaningless affair.'

He nodded. 'I know! Are you prepared to travel with me for a while? Kent is a nice chap; I'm sure you'll like him. We'll invite Pablo and Carmelita now and then, for old time's sake. I've already made enough money for us, our children and probably even for their children, but I still have the same driving ambition to be the best. Something has changed though — one thing is even more important to me than golf . . . that's you, and I want you to be happy.' He paused and sounded very serious. 'If you don't want to go on travelling, I'll gradually withdraw from the circuit.'

She cleared the lump in her throat and pretended not to be affected by the electricity of his touch. She discovered that even his fingertips on her skin had the power to stir her. She grinned. 'Can you guarantee that our bedroom will not be invaded by female fans?'

He chuckled. 'You have my personal blessings to throw any out! I seem to attract the wrong kind of people — but I swear you're the only woman for me now and forever. Just be there, that's all I ask of you.' He broke off, and his eyes smouldered briefly, before his mouth covered hers.

Emma had a burning desire, an aching need for him. His hands moved gently down the length of her back and she sighed involuntarily. 'Damián; I can't drop everything and come back. I have to finish my contract here.' Emma didn't know how she'd concentrate properly on listing books, but she would. 'Then I'll be able to make new plans.'

His eyes had a brilliant shine and he looked happier than she'd ever seen him. He nodded. 'I'll find somewhere to stay locally, play golf during the day, and after work you and I will start to get to know one another properly.'

His words registered and she met his

glance. With heightened colour and senses reeling, she nodded.

He was reassured and smiled broadly. 'You haven't actually answered me; will you come with me, will you marry me?'

She wrapped her arms around his neck; her heart was bursting with happiness. 'Yes, of course.' His arms tightened round her with steely strength and there was nothing in the world but the trees in the wind, the multi-coloured leaves swirling round their feet and Damián's body moulded to hers.

Damián Alvarez was a dynamic, unusual man. He'd never change — but she didn't want him to change. Behind that devil-may-care facade was a character she could rely on to help her weather the storms of life.

She loved him exactly as he was.

Other titles in the
Linford Romance Library:

THE POWER AND THE PASSION

Joyce Johnson

After a failed business venture and a broken engagement, artist Abbie Richards takes advantage of an opportunity to do a year's English teaching in Sicily. There, she becomes involved with the large, extended Puzzi family; it's members wealthy and powerfully placed in the community. Abbie enjoys the teaching and the social life at Maria Puzzi's language school, and falls in love with charismatic surgeon Roberto Puzzi, only to find herself dangerously entangled in the Puzzi power struggles . . .

HOLD ME CLOSE

Margaret Mounsdon

Resting actress Sara Armitage is thrilled to be offered a job, even if it means looking after Lyle Jackson's young daughter Jenny. Sara and Lyle have history and when Carla de Courcy, now Lyle's ex-wife and Jenny's mother, appears back on the scene, Sara is forced to face up to her past. Will Lyle break her heart for a second time or is she strong enough to withstand her love for him?